The Wish Store

BOOKS BY SHIRLEY BURTON

CHRISTMAS
Clockmaker's Christmas
Christmas Treasure Box
A Wenceslas Christmas
The Wish Store

HISTORICAL FICTION
Homage: Chronicles of a Habitant

THRILLERS
Don't Open the Door
Red Jackal
THOMAS YORK SERIES:
Under the Ashes - Book One
The Frizon - Book Two
Rogue Courier - Book Three
Secret Cache - Book Four
The Paris Network - Book Five
The Masquerade - Book Six

MYSTERY
Epitaph of an Imposter
Sentinel in the Moors
INSPECTOR FURNACE MYSTERIES:
Mystery at Grey Stokes
Swindle: Mystery at Sea

FANTASY
Boy from Saint-Malo

shirleyburtonbooks.com

The Wish Store

Shirley Burton

To Lynn,
Shirley Burton

HIGH STREET PRESS

HIGH STREET PRESS
Niagara-on-the-Lake, ON, Canada
highstreetpress.com
shirleyburtonbooks.com
First printing 2021

Printed in the United States of America, Canada, UK, Australia, and global distribution in Europe, Asia, and South America.
Available in paperback, hardcover, and eBook formats.
Cover photo licensed Shutterstock.com.
Design and edit: Bruce Burton

Library and Archives Canada Cataloguing in Publication.

Burton, Shirley, 1950-, author
        A Wenceslas Christmas/ Shirley Burton

Issued in print and electronic versions.
ISBN 978-1-927839-42-3 (pbk.). —ISBN 978-1-927839-43-0 (hardcover)
ISBN 978-1-927839-44-7 (ebook)

This story is inspired by and dedicated to my son Michael, who I am sure is an elf in disguise. Christmas is truly in our hearts and in helping others no matter what age we are. It is not what you get but what you give that builds memories. Elves are like angels, and you will encounter them when least expected.

CAST OF CHARACTERS

Rev. Atkins, local church pastor
Mr. Baylor, mail delivery
Carl Bench, radio announcer
Mandy Carson, child posting letter to Santa
Clarence Fairhill, violinist band member
Philip Graber, benefactor, a tourist from Stowe
Maeve Grissom, long time clerk at Emporium
Micah, a senior part-time elf at Emporium
Gabriella Hancock, Rudy's daughter
Gary Hancock, Rudy's son
Rudy Hancock, owner of Hancock's Emporium
Sadie Hancock, Rudy's wife, runs the café
Walter Hoskins, hardware store owner
William Jackson, private in Iraq
Ewan Leadner, Mayor of Chimney Ridge, Fezziwig
Mrs. Leadner, Mrs. Fezziwig
Cyril Metcalf family, residents of Chimney Ridge
Myrtle Middleton, organizer of Fezziwig Ball
Nate Newman, ex-military fulfilling Mandy's wish
Henry Parker, Lola's newspaper boy
Eleanor Partridge, Chimney Ridge shopper
Bradley Rimble, a homeless lad, becomes an elf
Keith Rimble, bandleader
Benedict (Dick) Thompson, a past recipient of Deed
Lydia Thompson, single mother, nurse
Lola Turnbull, an aged resident, resigned to care home
Clifford Winters, lonely widower & Rudy's neighbor

1

H owling winds swirled across the mountain terrain at Chimney Ridge, with blinding snow obscuring the rooftops and landmark chimneys. Crisp blankets covered the hills and valleys that converged into the idyllic, sleepy town nestled in the Green Mountains of Vermont.

Clapboard federal-style buildings heralding New England's history lined the boulevards with saltboxes and brick and stone colonial structures renovated for the twentieth century.

As their window lights flickered, the chimneys puffed and circled into the night sky over the deserted street.

Tonight, on the eve of December, the drifts sweeping downtown waited for no one as the storm swallowed the muffled gongs of Memorial Park's town clock as it struck midnight.

Midway down the main route was Hancock's Emporium,

a time-honored landmark that stood out from the rest of the shops, especially in December, with a vision to create Christmas magic for the town of Chimney Ridge. Tall, atrium-style windows and fretted panes were decorated with bulbs and baubles to invite villagers to peer into the store's secrets in the morning. Over the front door, the hanging sign creaked and swayed in the wind.

On this November 30th night, Rudy Hancock, the proprietor, and his wife, Sadie, were warm and cozy in their second-floor apartment above the Emporium, sheltered from the snowstorm.

Generations of Hancocks before them had passed forward this passion for stirring the festive spirit that now revolved for twelve months of the year to prepare for the upswing to Christmas.

As she scooped their second helpings of Shepherd's Pie, he reset the tape of Bing Crosby crooning, 'I'm Dreaming of a White Christmas.'

"You know, the sentiment comes from being a kid, back to my family being together," Sadie reminded Rudy.

As she reminisced, her memory flashed back to Crown Point, New York. "I've always loved snow at Christmas," she said. We tobogganed near the Fort packed in snowsuits, the eight of us. We were a large family." She giggled as her eyes opened wide. "Oh, yes; you know *all* about that."

"Yes, yes, I've heard it before!" Rudy teased as she'd expect whenever she reminisced. "Eight of you huddled around the hearth in a log cabin,"

"Quit your mocking, and turn up the news!"

The black Motorola tube radio crackled on the mahogany sideboard as the newscaster reported a storm warning. Rudy twisted the tuner dial to rid the static and turned up the volume on the gravelly radio voice of Carl Bench, a long-time local reporter.

"This is a weather warning for tonight and tomorrow, the first of December. Temperatures will fall below freezing until the early hours, and anyone outside should take shelter. Police report cars in the ditch and advise against travel. Winds are over 40 miles per hour with eight inches of snow expected before morning."

Rudy scanned the street from his window. "Eight inches? It's that much already!"

The shops were closed, and the streams of white drifts had begun to pack up against entrances in his sight.

"Hear that wind now?" Sadie said. "It's shrill like a whistle. But even if it snows all night, we can't slow down. Tomorrow the town celebrates, and we'll have to be ready to set out the Wish Boxes for the town."

"That's true. Kids will be writing their treasured letters at this very moment tonight," said Rudy. "Even in a foot of snow, they'll be trudging to our North Pole post tomorrow."

He pulled back the curtain again to admire the scene. "Yesterday's paper says 'Miracle of 34th' was on channel three tonight. That'll spark even more excitement in the kids about Santa Claus."

"And faith in the letter system," Sadie said. "Nothing will stop the children, not even the harshest storm."

"We are so fortunate," said Rudy. "It's a privilege to do this, to help people and see the generous hearts of our townsfolk. We can realize their wishes, and they're always ready to pitch in to make others' dreams come true."

"Today, the kids in the store were giddy in anticipation."

"The eager ones will line up early at our door like last year.

I hope the roads and sidewalks get plowed in time," said Rudy.

"Remember the black and white TV movies when Gary and Gabriella were small when they concocted their creative twist on Night Before Christmas?"

"And the kids gave the bloodhound parts in their play?"

The two hooted at the image of the dog in a costume, and Sadie held up a wrinkled wrapping paper.

"Rudy, this was with the decorations. It's written in Gabriella's hand block letters on the back:

'Twas weeks before Christmas when all through the town,
Not a creature was stirring, not even our hound.
The elves were all busy making their toys,
For Santa to bring to good girls and boys.
Letters to Santa with a wish from the heart,
Not always a toy, but something apart.
A wish for a loved one to bless with a dream,
A reunion, companion, a friend, it would seem."

Rudy kissed her cheek as he refilled their coffee mugs. "There's more," she said.

"Blessings are never found under the tree,
But given by those who will always believe.
Believe in the spirit of wishes and deeds,
To bring joy and fresh spirit to all those in need."

As Sadie gathered dishes, Rudy stood at the window to assess the snow accumulating on the street below.

"It looks like a fantasy with the buildings caked with white icing," he said. "The flakes are becoming enormous, drifting now like fairies, landing on the lamppost boughs."

Sadie sidled up beside him. "Perhaps so much snow tonight is the best way for Christmas to come to Chimney Ridge. You always see the good in everything and everyone, Rudy; I'm glad of that."

She touched her finger to the pane. "Jack Frost left his artwork on the glass—see his etchings? My father said that no two snowflakes are the same, and our kids always looked for Jack Frost on the window, leading to the arrival of the jolly elf."

"I believe someone is down there in the bus shelter," said Rudy. He pressed his face to the glass, and Sadie squeezed closer. Then, side by side, with their hands blocking the window's reflection, they searched through the darkness for footprints or signs of anyone else.

"Poor fellow," said Rudy. "There's no bus at this hour of the day, and he mustn't have a place to sleep tonight."

At the top of the stairs, Rudy pulled on his wool toque hat. "I'll go and see who it is. It looks like we might have an overnight guest, Sadie!"

In his high boots, he tromped down the flight of stairs to the store below, and Sadie heard the rush of wind slam the door. As the chill blew up the stairs, she shuddered and pulled her sweater tight around her.

Bradley Rimble was twenty years old and had lived on the streets for the last two winters. Traveling through the New England states, he had found Stowe, Vermont, to his liking.

In his first summer in Stowe, he worked as a porter for the Von Trapp Lodge, but he looked for work in nearby towns as bookings thinned.

Finding odd jobs, he partook of meals at the soup kitchen on Barbary Road in Chimney Ridge, staying after the late servings to wash dishes and delaying a homeless night.

Unfortunately, Bradley remained at the meal program late this night after the church had closed, and he was without a bed and warmth.

Stepping out of the mission kitchen, he was stunned to walk into the gale that had descended on them. His light jacket billowed up like a flying kite as the winds surged up his sleeves.

Hardly able to feel his toes, he headed toward a string of lights for security, hoping that some folks lived over the shops on the main street.

He'd learned to stuff newspapers into his shoes and to use cardboard for a bed and blankets, but tonight's temperature was dropping rapidly, and the strength of the gale made it challenging to breathe.

Following the lampposts, he took refuge in a glass structure at the first bus stop.

With the force of the wind, Rudy pulled his scarf over his face and plodded toward the shelter. As his eyes adjusted to the moonlight, he focused on the shape huddled in the corner of the enclosed lean-to.

"Hello! Is somebody here?" Rudy called, but his words whipped back into the wind.

From a struggle under some cardboard, a weak voice replied, "Over here. I'll be fine, and I don't mean to bother anyone."

"It's no bother, fellow. Come with me, I insist. I'm across the road; my house is warm, and the coffee is hot."

Bradley was too weak and disoriented to object. Rudy held out his hand to grasp the jacket of the skinny lad.

"Take hold of my sleeve and stick with me. We have

about sixty feet to go, but visibility is bad, so don't let go; I know my way in the dark."

Bradley had strands of icicles on his brows, and he could barely feel his nose or fingers. Rudy shoved a scarf into the lad's hands. "Hold this over your mouth so you can breathe."

"Yes, sir, thanks."

The lanky boy struggled to his feet, already numb. He followed Rudy's instructions and gripped the back of Hancock's coat as they forged through the wind to the light filtering from across the street. Leaning into the blizzard's force, the two heaved themselves forward.

In the distance, Rudy saw glimpses of the spires through the gusts. A muffled gong reverberated from the town's bell tower with its echo sounding far away, but it gave him the comfort he was near home.

At the Emporium's doorway, Sadie, an angel of mercy, stood with a rescue blanket ready and a battery torch waiting to light their steps. She called out, but her words were eaten into the storm.

Ten feet from the doorway, Rudy gripped the stranger's hand. "We're here; you're safe now."

Sadie had scraped away enough snow to open the front door of the Emporium. She gathered the shuddering boy with a blanket around his lean body and light overcoat. He paused at the floor, wondering if he should wipe his feet.

"My goodness, you're frozen solid."

She tightened the blanket around his shoulders and embraced him as if he were her son.

"Come inside the store to thaw out first. Then can you make it upstairs?" asked Rudy. "That's where we live."

"Thanks. It got wicked pretty fast. I didn't expect the

storm, and I missed the deadline to sleep in the church basement."

Surprisingly, Rudy's voice boomed with glee. "It's not a storm, son; it's a Christmas miracle."

"What could be good about this weather?" Bradley thought to himself.

"I'll get you warmed up," Sadie said, and her nature took hold to mother the stray boy.

Bradley didn't resist but gasped at the sight, standing inside this magical place. It smelled of pine, cinnamon, cloves, and everything Christmassy.

The shelves overflowed with handmade wooden toys, colorful creations, felt stockings, decorations, wreaths, trees, tinsel garlands, festive lanterns, and bundles of red and gold bells.

In the corner, he encountered a trio of stuffed elves of all sizes and a life-size version of Father Christmas, then a row of brightly colored, carved nutcrackers, and a collection of hand-painted Dickens carolers. The night lighting shed enough glow on their faces to remind him of his childhood.

"This must be the North Pole!" he said with a hesitant laugh.

"Almost, kid. Come upstairs, and we'll get you settled," said Rudy, "and I'll explain where you are."

In the living room, the woodstove crackled, and the room exuded a warmth of spirit that Bradley hadn't known since he left home two years before. Sadie bustled about with hot chocolate and her apple pie, while Rudy found him a flannel plaid shirt and heavy work socks.

"Pull a chair up by the stove and thaw your feet. Here, lad, you get comfortable, and we'll have a chat."

"My name is Bradley Rimble."

"It's a pleasure. I'm Rudy Hancock, and this is my wife, Sadie. Tell us about yourself."

"I've been wandering for a few years, but at this moment, I can't think of the reason. I've worked odd jobs in surrounding communities, but nothing permanent. Sometimes time passes, and now I don't remember why I had a spat with my father. I recall storming out the door of our house, slamming the door, and promising myself that I would never return."

Bradley's head lowered, feeling a mixture of shame and regret.

"We own the Emporium and this building," said Rudy. "Our son and daughter are at college but will be home for Christmas. If one of them had stomped out the door in anger for any reason, I would cherish the day of their return."

Bradley's eyes widened at the words.

"I expect that is how your father feels as well," Rudy said.

In this strange environment, Bradley relaxed his shoulders and allowed himself to be at ease for the first time in ages as he listened in silence to Rudy's advice.

"Forgiveness is an incredible gift," Rudy continued, "and pride is the thorn of our inner selves. I hope you will find the difference when you are ready."

Bradley quietly observed the store's surroundings with its decorations, aromas, and the spirit it represented. Rudy's carpentry skills were immediately apparent, and Bradley nodded toward a hanging advent calendar that took up the wall above the sideboard.

"Did you build and carve that?"

"I did indeed," said Rudy with pride.

"Can you show me how it works?

"Starting tomorrow, December first, every day has a hand-painted character that's activated by springs. A timer is set for six every morning to open the doors for that day."

"Come to the table near the stove and warm yourself," Sadie interrupted. "Don't mind me as I'll listen from here. I'm baking for the morning tearoom."

An assortment of mugs, plates, and mixing bowls was already on the kitchen table, and on the counter, she deposited an orchestra of pots and pans from the cupboards, bowls from the pantry, and sacks of flour and sugar.

"I'd like to help."

"Thanks, Bradley, but I have a system on the go for the moment."

"I'm curious," Rudy mused. "I try to get to know everyone in our lovely town, and I assist at the mission kitchen when it's possible. So I'm remiss that I've overlooked you somehow."

Bradley flushed with embarrassment at his reclusive behavior and that he had avoided getting to know people.

"I confess I'm a loner and gravitate to an obscure escape. The folks in town have been very kind to me, and I owe them a debt of gratitude."

He wrapped his hands around the warm mug, and a sloppy sip left a marshmallow mustache on his lip. "I haven't done that since I was a kid!" He wiped his sleeve across his mouth, cracking his first grin.

"You know, Bradley, you have come here tonight for a reason." Rudy's face shone as he spoke. "We're not the North Pole you read about in storybooks, but for many folks in Chimney Ridge, this is the store where dreams and wishes come true at Christmas."

Bradley's eyes darted around the room as he slid forward to the chair's edge. "I'd like to hear more."

"We believe in the magic of Christmas," said Rudy, "and the people of this good town."

"And I suppose you have a workshop somewhere here with elves that are building toys and stuffing red sacks," Bradley said.

"That's pretty close to the truth. You see, my father, who we called Pops, was a carpenter, and for years, he made Christmas toys and other delights. Soon, he had a name throughout New England for his craftsmanship."

"That's quite a reputation."

"Yes, but unfortunately, years ago, he passed away after a heart attack. I was the oldest of four, and it was my duty to take over his craft with his tools and benches. I sense his presence each time I pick up his instruments or sit where he sat. If I wait, his inspiration comes to me too.

"This marvelous town of Chimney Ridge honored Pops by naming the first of December as a day of celebration that ushers in the season of Wishes and Dreams."

"Tomorrow? Is that the start of Wishes and Dreams?

"Indeed it is; tonight's the eve of December, so you're here just in time."

"Is your workshop here, sir?"

"Oh, yes! In the basement. The Emporium is the portal to the North Pole for all the children in town, and the elves work in the imaginary workshop they envision in their dreams. As I said, you are not here by accident."

Rudy watched Bradley's expression change as he slowly became a believer in his fate at arriving in this enchanting place. He grinned to himself, wondering for a moment if Santa Claus might genuinely be here.

Over a checkers match, Rudy began his fascinating stories about the giving nature of the citizens of Chimney Ridge.

"Christmas is what you want it to be," he said. "That's what the community believes. Benevolence has become part of the town, and we thrive on it."

"I've barely arrived, Mr. Hancock, so what if anything can I do?"

"There's so much enjoyable work to be done. It begins in the heart," said Rudy.

"I don't get it," Bradley admitted as he grappled with the concept.

"Christmas starts in the heart; it's better to look after others, to be charitable than to receive. It builds character too. And, by the way, I'm Rudy to all my friends."

Bradley sat in stunned silence, absorbing the words. "I don't know what to say, Rudy."

"That is why *you* are here. Every year on the eve of December, someone finds us and becomes an elf. You are not here by accident. Have a good night's rest as tomorrow you will become an elf."

2

Rudy's Motivation

The morning aroma of Sadie's coffee lured Bradley from his bed, and when he ventured into the kitchen, the sight astonished him, with tray after tray of muffins, scones, tarts, cupcakes, and gingerbread characters.

A man in a red sweater was hunched over the woodstove stoking the embers. He was greying at his temples, but his elfish ears and rosy cheeks only added to his jovial appearance.

Bradley rubbed his eyes as if in a dream, and when he opened wide again, he still felt awkward at his entrance into the good Samaritan's sanctuary.

"Good morning, Rudy."

"Ah, I was about to go and get you. It's the first of December, and it brings us so much work to do!"

Rudy's enthusiasm filled the kitchen, and he looked up

quizzically. "You do believe in elves, don't you?"

"About elves? Every child knows about Santa's helpers. How else could those toys get made and loaded onto the sleigh?"

Bradley realized his words were nervous and meandering, and he tried to be entertaining. "I suppose you have reindeer somewhere in town too!"

"Ah, you still need some convincing, I see."

The first door was open at the advent calendar, and a miniature carpenter working at his bench caught Bradley's scrutiny. He stepped close and ran his fingers over the fine details. "It's extraordinary. I'm sorry I missed the chime when the doors opened."

"It's the anticipation, don't you think?"

"I remember that feeling as a boy, the first time seeing my train set pulling out of the station my dad built. Its movement was so real to me."

"That was the same with my father years ago. He was a true craftsman, and I only hope to be that good one day. If at times we can follow in a master's footsteps, it can make the blueprint easier."

"I admire your craft, Rudy, and even more your passion for what you are doing."

"I hope you will remember your own words, Bradley. Have a bite, and then I'll take you down to the carpentry shop. Our special boxes will begin to come to life again as they become a reality for another Christmas. This place will be a hub of activity today with volunteers."

"I'm ready if you tell me where to start."

"I'm glad to hear that. Take a gander and choose where you'd like to pitch in. But, first, check at the writing desk in the living room. Front and center is the agenda calendar that keeps us on track for the next few weeks."

Hearing them, Sadie returned with bundles of wrapping paper. "Besides hosting customers at the Emporium, my favorite is the Fezziwig Ball in a fortnight."

"Oh, yes. Sadie at the Fezziwig!" Rudy let out an infectious roar of laughter that got them joining in. "I think you'll be surprised to find that she is indeed the belle of the ball on that night. Everyone in town surges into the community hall. It's the event of the season, an evening you won't forget."

"Fezziwig?" Bradley repeated. "How soon is that?"

"Two weeks. By the time it comes around, our daughter Gabriella will be home." He winked at Bradley. "And if I may be presumptuous, she'd like an escort."

Dreaming about the ball, Sadie blushed. "I do enjoy the dressing-up part. I ordered a fancy ball gown with lace and crinolines from England years back, the best place to find Charles Dickens costumes. Of course, it's the same dress every year, but we create so much fun.

"And about Gabriella, Rudy is teasing you; her dance card will fill up faster than a mouse after cheese. Our family picture is there on the bureau if you'd like to see it."

Bradley looked perplexed, taking in the whirlwind morning. "I'm puzzled as I don't know anything about a Fezziwig Ball."

"You must be aware of the fabled Dickens Christmas Carol. The ghost of Christmas Past took Scrooge to the Fezziwig grand ball for his friends and employees. I'm sure it will come back to you."

"I know that one. Young Ebenezer was his prize employee in his early days! Fezziwig was the epitome of everything Scrooge lost sight of and represented charity."

"Exactly, and goodwill," said Rudy. "Old Fezziwig knew how to have a good time and had his friends share in the frivolity. We think ours is the most fun you could ever imagine."

"Look over the calendar," said Sadie. "We are back-to-back with activities and responsibilities."

"Our son, Gary, will come a week before Christmas to pitch in," Rudy said, "and Gabriella a few days earlier. It's all hands on deck to get to Christmas Eve. It sounds exhausting, but it's quite magnificent."

Sadie's motherly instinct noticed Bradley's confusion. "We'll make you comfortable. Your room has twin beds, and Gary will bunk in with you. We can't afford to lose any elves before Christmas."

"The sleep last night was the best in months. I assure you I'm comfortable!"

"A few ladies and students from town will come and go through the store for a few hours here and there. We have the food bank drive, a charity bake sale, and a box lunch auction."

Rudy interrupted, "Don't forget the carol parades!"

"Oh yes," Sadie said. "And every Sunday, the church does a nativity play; next week, we'll take stockings to the old folks' homes and help the animal shelter promote an adoption event—."

Sadie paused again for a breath, and Rudy jumped in. "As you'll be here until Christmas, Bradley, you could make a big impact in the Wishes and Deeds. The town counts on us to make the impossible possible, so it's a serious commitment."

Bradley stirred with anticipation, and his uncertain future was put at ease with Rudy's assurance that he'd be here until Christmas.

"Wishes and Deeds? I've never heard of this type of conspiracy," he joked.

"We base ambitions on faith and patience. You'll understand."

"The sign outside says the Emporium was established in 1791," Bradley said. "Is the building historical?"

"If you've been to the town hall, you'll have seen that the community honors our forebearers with portraits. Even our souvenir shops have books about ancestors. It's claimed that the Declaration of Independence signatory, John Hancock, is a remote relative of mine. That even sometimes creates tourist curiosity."

"Really! I didn't connect that. But, of course, everyone knows about John Hancock."

"There are many historic towns around Vermont, and it was told that Rudyard Kipling sojourned nearby when he made a stopover from the stagecoach. You could listen to the old folks for hours telling tales of colonial days, but you'd never know for sure if they were authentic."

"There are others, with the Vermont Rangers led by Samuel Herrick and a suggestion that George Washington himself overnighted at the Musket & Thistle. Legend says he was in town to conscript hundreds of acres of wheat to supply the militia at Bennington. Other towns in New England have similar claims, and no one is alive to refute them."

"The Hancock family reference must make you proud."

"When folks ask, I say that many came on the Mayflower or to other settlements. Regardless, generations lay claim to our American heritage through their toiling and service. But we must admit that the land belonged to indigenous caretakers who didn't complain too loudly. It is best to agree that God blessed us all. I found that would baffle many discussions."

"When did the Emporium stake a hold on your Christmas Wishes and Deeds?"

"Ah, my grandfather passed the mission on to my father, Pops. This quaint historic town was always a paradise of privacy, and the opportunities waited."

"For tourists, you mean . . ."

"More than that. True, we're renowned for the snow-capped mountains of Stowe and Spruce's Peak that bring tourists for adventure and a cozy cabin. It keeps many employed.

"But one day, Pops decided that Christmas was bigger than skiing, and he enticed the good people of Chimney Ridge into his plan."

"Was the Fezziwig Ball in his original idea?"

"Not at first. We came up with the theme when I was a teenager watching Scrooge one night. It came to us like a lightbulb. When Ebenezer's employer became overcome with generosity, we decided that Fezziwig could be contagious in our small town."

3

Gearing Up for Parade Day

Nestled in the Adirondacks, Chimney Ridge was built around old lumber and grist mills established on the tributary of the Richelieu River that flowed northward to the St. Lawrence and Lake Champlain of the Ohio Valley. After the Revolution, Vermont was the fourteenth American colony, clustered on the Quebec border, wedged between New York, New Hampshire, and Massachusetts.

The town maintained its charm as it grew with general stores, taverns, century buildings converted into shops, and cafes lining its streets. Whenever big-city chain stores or restaurants applied to venture into empty spaces, the council rejected their proposals, preserving its historical elements and fearing the burden of expansion and too much prosperity.

The clock ticked slowly and loudly as Rudy tossed through the night, staring at the ceiling, imagining the setup for the magical boxes awaiting in the basement workshop. Over the years, as he aged, the anticipation had never faded.

The alarm woke him at five, and he jumped from his bed pumped up with adrenalin.

Rudy dressed appropriately for the parade and the official launch of the Wishes and Deeds boxes. In a festive red cardigan over his crisp white shirt, green suspenders, and candy cane print bowtie, he patted his belly, aware he'd put on a few pounds in hopes of making a suitable presentation in the Santa suit on Christmas Eve.

Hearing Bradley in the kitchen, he was heartened to have his help. He'd never really offered Bradley a job or room and board but assumed they were pieces of his puzzle that would fall in place.

Bradley's head popped around to peer in from the hallway. The wall clock said five to six, and he watched for the spring to release for day two.

Pop, Spring, Grind, Tap, Tap. Then in a sudden halt, a pair of miniature doors released and expelled a toy workbench with two tiny elves tapping hammers. Bradley grinned broadly, enamored at the calendar's transaction, then stood as his imagination lingered, wanting more.

At his sight, Rudy's baritone voice boomed, "Ah, ha! It is our parade day. The town is decked with boughs, and the colored lights are on all day."

"I'm ready and rested!" said Bradley. "What happens and how soon?"

"It's indeed a special day," Rudy said. "A parade of festooned horses with carriages will trot through town and into the skating arena. Then, this afternoon, folks will line the main street to watch a variety of colorful floats, waving and singing to the band."

"It sounds like a movie," Bradley said.

"But even more than that. Behind the floats, folks will promenade on the streets with festivity, dancing jigs, with arms locked together in celebration. No cues or rehearsals, just instinct."

"As the town grows, does it stay the same every year?"

Rudy angled his head. "That's a wise question about change. A spill-over of tourists encroaches on the outer limits of the town; you know where the new apartment buildings are under construction next to the expansion of the retirement lodge?"

Bradley didn't know where but nodded. "You sound like you regret that. Does it have to be a bad thing?"

"Our citizens like doing things the old way, like collecting gossip on the main street. The town is teaching the high students about computers, but I'll have none of it—it's a foreign language to me."

"Rudy, in time, it will become a way of life; this is the eighties, and you can't stop progress. Someday, you'll need to do business on the internet; you'll place orders and track services. Your customers will expect that."

"Sounds ironic to me, Bradley. Look at history, how the explorers traveled, and battles were fought; they used scouts, signals, maps, and the bravest even ran through the woods. What about our own Captain Thomas Johnston? He led his minutemen during the Revolution without a computer, and we survived."

They both laughed, knowing that Rudy wouldn't budge. "You've thrived just fine without change," Bradley said, "so I won't suggest anything different. You have a vision, but most of all, the biggest heart I've ever seen!"

"Come along to the store's basement," Rudy said as he led the way. "Down here, I set up Pops' carpentry bench where I fashion toys and unique items for the store."

A glow from below lit up the staircase as they reached the lower steps. "The colors are fascinating," said Bradley.

"Ah, yes, the workshop is exactly that with its beautiful creations; it's a cornucopia, to be sure. Anyone seeing them would envision the pleasure the crafts will bring to others."

"Handmade puppets too," said Bradley. "Pinocchio!"

"Look at my repertoire of puppets and marionettes: Not just Pinocchio, but Peter Rabbit, Howdy Dowdy, Captain Hook, Mary Poppins, Papa Gigio, and others. So naturally, as the demand for these figures grew over the years, the workshop flourished."

Bradley rotated in a pirouette to take in the menagerie, becoming almost dizzy in the fantasy.

"I spend hours daily crafting in this winter workshop from Labor Day. Pops taught me at his elbow to plane and sand. His drawings of old-world style patterns were endless, to preserve folklore and fictional characters that children adore." Rudy grinned at his recollection. "Children of all ages, I say."

"It's a legacy your dad left, and you've continued it," Bradley said.

"When it comes my time to go to the Pearly Gates, I want to be either at my bench or the Fezziwig Ball, ha-ha."

Two ancient boxes waited on a shelf over his workbench with etchings carved into the wood—Wishes and Deeds. Each small trunk revealed a delicately crafted winter motif that received a fresh paint touch-up every year, a bit of sanding, and an occasional shellacking for new gloss when needed.

Sadie's voice echoed from the staircase. "Breakfast, boys! You'll need energy for what's ahead."

She'd warmed up the oven before the sun rose and the baking aromas drifted through the apartment.

"It'll be a fabulous day!" Sadie proclaimed. "I just know it!" She wiped her hands on her apron, and despite her upswept hair askew from her kitchen labor's haste, she looked radiant.

Rudy wrapped his arms around her waist and pressed his cheek against hers. "Good morning, love. I can't wait to get started."

"Then pour some coffee and dig into these hot biscuits with my strawberry jam. That'll hold you."

Aware of the tasks ahead, she asked Bradley to carry trays down to the café. "The mince tarts will come out of the oven; then the candied shortbread can go in. Set the timer for ten minutes."

"Mmm, we ate my grandmother's mince tarts around the Christmas tree—." He stopped himself from remembering out loud. "I'll be right behind you, Mrs. Hancock."

Rudy had renovated the atrium into a café at the back of the Emporium, necessary as customers lingered in long neighborly conversations. In time, it was named Sadie's Place, where folks could meet and chat while consuming baked goods.

Sadie insisted on propriety in choosing teacups, saucers, and English china plates if the café carried her name. "Remember to put out the prettiest china, not those cafeteria ones that Micah brought in."

"Rest assured, Mrs. Hancock; I'll deliver every tray

downstairs as they're out of the oven."

She wiped her brow with a napkin. "Thank you, dear boy, and I'm used to being called Sadie. The glass pastry cases are empty, but these will fill them. After the next timer, I'll be along."

In no time, Bradley was shuttling between Sadie's kitchen and the café. They already depended on him, and he recognized this new sense of belonging.

Clifford Winters, an aged veteran, lived in a primitive cottage off the main route in Settler's Row., He had grown up in the house as an only child and built a shoe repair shack on the side. Clifford was suffering from loneliness, as he had lost his wife last year.

It was still dark as he lay in bed, and the silence was deafening as there was no Thelma bustling about or kettle whistling, no floorboards creaking, and no warm spot beside him. He knew he must escape the remorseful feeling of being a widower that overtook him every morning.

He could see the top of the bell tower and the peaked turret roof at the back of Rudy's Emporium from his upstairs window.

While chimneys across town were puffing bright smoke wisps from their hearths, he felt a contrast of emptiness, but even these few minutes connecting with his neighborhood briefly lifted his spirits. After his sleepless night, it gave him comfort to see Rudy's apartment lights and the garret's pre-dawn glow.

Clifford and Thelma Winters had been active in a social circle until she became ill. Well-wishers brought casseroles and good wishes, but when she could not get up, they stopped coming. So he converted the music room into a bedroom and added a main floor bathroom to make her more comfortable. Now he kept that sliding door closed and rarely entered.

With his spirits low, he grumbled about his demise, keeping it inside. "It's awkward like I am a contagious invalid," he said aloud. "Like I've lost my right arm. But there's no value in pitying myself."

The well-meaning townsfolk were slow to adapt to Cliff's widowhood and embrace him in this new status.

He was tall and broad-shouldered and spry for his age and accustomed to walks through downtown as his daily routine. In his morning excursions, he regularly stopped in with his infectious good morning to Rudy, bearing a gregarious demeanor and a routine joke remembered from the morning paper.

On December first, Clifford trudged through the snowdrifts before the street shops opened and was the first to appear at Rudy's. The bells jingling over the Emporium's threshold had been there from long before it was a hardware store and announced Cliff's arrival.

Cliff made his opening jab as the bells echoed to the back.

"Knock, knock," he called out.

"Who's there?" Rudy bantered with his grin spread ear to ear.

"Tree."

"Tree Who?"

"Tree Wise Men," Cliff said with a squeaky snort before it sputtered out into a snicker. "It's not my joke, Rudy; it was in the paper."

"I could have guessed, pal."

Clifford hushed at the sight of a new face beside Rudy and Sadie, the young lad now also dressed in a red cardigan crested with 'Rudy's Emporium.' He was accustomed to new faces showing up in the Hancock household and nodded his approval of the unknown elf.

"For a cup of coffee, I'll shovel your walk, Rudy," he said. "Winter arrived in full force during the night."

"Naw, Clifford, you can't shovel, but you can make the coffee while I give it a go. I have a helper starting today that I'm training to be an elf. Meet Bradley Rimble."

Bradley's handshake shot out, and he stepped smartly across the room.

"Meet Clifford Winters," Rudy said. "He's my pal. And Clifford, the town already ran their sidewalk plow along, so there's not much to clear, and the rest will melt before noon."

Cliff knew his way around the store and doffed his hat and coat in the backroom, and began his routine lighting the gas burner. As the percolator worked up its rhythm, he set out the food bank baskets and turned on the tree lights.

"Well, Sadie, I smell home baking," he teased as she walked by to her café. "So good!"

"Wouldn't something be wrong if you didn't? We've been up since dawn. Help yourself with my peach cream cheese muffins. Yes, they're still warm."

As Winters ambled toward the café alcove, two more clerks arrived through the front door and to the task list. In no time, they were attired in festive aprons and bustling through the store.

The first was a local church member, Micah, an ambitious worker who treasured his annual Christmas stint at the Emporium. With sleeves rolled to the elbows, he began unpacking and stocking shelves and toy displays.

The second arrival, a middle-aged grandmother, Maeve

Grissom, gave a headshake of approval to the recruit, ready to take charge of his training.

"I ran into Rudy outside, Bradley; he tells me you are in training. We'll transform this magnificent shop into the North Pole in no time and get you looking fully like the elf you've become."

Humbled by the overwhelming attention, he instinctively picked up a broom and scurried to sweep out the snow footprints that had arrived in the store.

4

The First Letter Posted

Returning inside from the cold frosty air, Rudy shook the chunks of snow off his boots, invigorated by winter's overnight arrival. He yanked off the scarf and flap-eared cap and tossed them onto a hook behind the door.

He looked his friend directly in the eye. "Clifford, I couldn't sleep last night for thinking about all there is to do."

"I know; I saw that your light was on upstairs. It's my first Christmas without Thelma, and I've got to find my spirit and go on. She would want that." He knew there wasn't a need to explain, but it felt good to say it.

"Thelma will be missed in Sadie's tearoom. The two of them made those funnel cakes and sugar cookies."

Rudy looked up as he spoke, but seeing the pain on Clifford's face, he regretted bringing up these memories.

"I've lost a few pounds this year," Cliff uttered, lost in thought as if he were somewhere else.

But something caught Rudy's eye, and he watched the old gent with interest, admiring how much he looked like Santa Claus, with snowy-white curly hair and a few days of white and grey scruff on his chin.

Typically, when in reflection, Clifford's thumbs tucked into the straps of his favorite plaid suspenders, the intended antics of a grandfather.

"It just hit me, Cliff; I know what you need. When you drove the Sunday School bus in the past, the kids loved you. I know you will always bring happiness to a child's face."

"That was long ago, but it seems like yesterday." His face brightened. "It was the kids' laughter I liked the best. They loved to whoop it up in the bus."

"With so many events now, I can't be in two places at the same time," Rudy said, raising his eyes over his glasses for a reaction.

"Spill your mischief, Rudy. What do you need?"

"It's the nativity pageant at the church before Christmas. Give Santa Claus a thought, and we'll talk about it again soon."

Rudy watched the twinkle in Clifford's eye, envisioning himself in the red suit, hearing the whispers of children's secret wishes. Over the years, Cliff and Thelma had cooed over the church youngsters, although they were never blessed with their own.

Sadie overheard the suggestion and understood the plan afoot. She never thought it was right for widows and widowers not to be matched up. "Just a waste of good people, I say."

Clifford settled into his regular spot in Sadie's café and nursed another coffee, pondering Rudy's scenarios. Lingering, he was avoiding the return to his lonely house.

Mandy Carson lived with her parents and two siblings at Hampstead Row, on the town's outskirts. The family recently returned from a road trip to New York to visit her grandparents and see the Macy's parade.

But a sadness stirred in the young girl. A nagging problem persisted with her, something only the great man in the North Pole could fix.

Her obsession was over her annual letter to be sent to Santa Claus. However, she persisted with her intention and her determination.

"I know he will do it; I just know."

The early mail was due at eight o'clock, and Mandy watched by the window for the square postal van driven by Mr. Baylor, the one with a loud muffler. Knowing she watched every day, he waved as he pulled up to the row of mailboxes with bundles of envelopes and magazines.

Across the street from the Carson's was a widowed military veteran, Mr. Jackson, a tall and lean man with a gimpy gait from shrapnel wounds from the Vietnam war.

Every morning, he waited too for Baylor's arrival, not for bills nor Christmas cards, but the scrawl of his son on a piece of mail. William was far away serving his country on the battlefields.

Mandy was aware that the military jeep arrived at Jackson's house last Christmas, and everyone knew what that dreaded vehicle meant. The green camouflage truck had come to an abrupt halt, and two uniformed officers approached. Jackson's two sons were serving in the Iraq-Iran war, and casualties were mounting every day.

The officers stood at attention and saluted, and he knew

what to expect. He didn't care much for the honor in a moment like that as he was readying his broken heart.

Mr. Jackson had nearly crumpled to the ground on the news that his son, Barry, was a pilot in a Black Hawk chopper struck by rocket fire with no survivors. An official document, a fistful of dog tags, and a folded flag were all that was left, with the assurance that a posthumous medal for his sacrifice and heroism would be forthcoming. The promise of a place for him in Arlington just left an open wound in his heart.

Mandy watched that morning and felt a pain she had not yet known in her eight years. Despair is not something a child usually experiences so young in life, especially not in Chimney Ridge. Soon after, she struck up a compassionate and endearing friendship with old Mr. Jackson.

He began to brighten seeing her return from school, skipping down the sidewalk to run to him. She let him talk and tell her about his two sons, their childhood adventures and dreams.

"You know, Barry is resting with heroes at Arlington Cemetery; I hear a flame burns there for a President, day and night. My William is younger than Barry but just as brave.

"I pray nightly for William's safety and return, Mandy. Perhaps you could, too. It's been a whole year, and Christmas is another reminder of that tragic, senseless loss. I find it hard."

Jackson pulled out a worn, wallet-sized photo of William in uniform. "He's so much like you, Mr. Jackson," Mandy said in her soft voice, and he nodded with a tear at the sensitivity of her young age. "Mom says I look a lot like my Dad, too."

After that, every night at bedtime, Mandy said a prayer

for William's safe return.

The Jackson house was quiet this year without its past decorations, and Mandy knew the painful reason. She wanted him to have Christmas spirit and smile again. Taking notepaper from the hall desk, she went to her room.

"Mom, can we go into the Emporium today," Mandy asked Mrs. Carson, who was in the kitchen with her holiday preparations. "I have a letter for the North Pole mailbox. There's something important I need to ask for, and it must make the mail as soon as possible. It can't be found in any store, but I must ask anyway."

"Sure, Mandy. I have a bundle of several dozen Christmas mittens ready for the Emporium in every size and color. Mr. Hancock said I could put them on consignment over the holidays like last year. Can you gather a tote from my sewing room?"

Mandy knew how hard her mother worked to provide for her and her sister and brother.

"I'm so proud; your mittens are the finest in Chimney Ridge, Mom. I think Mr. Hancock will especially like the ones with Rudolph on them as it's his name too. The colors are gorgeous, but my favorite is the snowman on bright blue!"

Mrs. Carson's pride was reciprocal, and she beamed at her daughter's thoughtful nature. "Stuey is at a sleepover, and Nancy is getting ready for a birthday party today, so it's just the two of us." Mandy skipped, away eager to help.

With the Emporium traffic already humming, Rudy focused on the Wish Boxes waiting in the workshop. Readjusting some tables and display boxes, he cleared the showcase closest to the store's front door. It had to be the right spot to suit him, like getting comfortable in bed at night.

"Alright, Bradley, let's go and get them," he said with a jab at the elf's shoulder.

"Ready."

Bradley's curiosity was growing about the mysterious basement workshop, and a shiver of anticipation ran up his spine as he descended the stairs.

His senses came alive at the top of the staircase, with the smell of seasonal fresh-cut pine, peppermint candy canes, and workshop scents of sawdust and paints.

Then the sounds, as he imagined the tapping of elves building toys, then an energetic chanting of Jingle Bells in a harmonic chorus of tiny voices. Finally, he absentmindedly began whistling along.

Rudy was a few steps ahead and joined in, with his arms swinging with energy and rhythm. Seconds later, he burst into the song.

A carpenter's bench spanned the wall under an overhead rack of planes, hand saws, carving tools, drills, paints, and varnishes. Shelves overflowed with wooden toys and innovations, exactly as Bradley had imagined the elves' workshop would be.

"Bradley, this is where wishes and dreams will be fulfilled. Anyone can bring in their own card or write one out here in the store and deposit it. On the parchment cards from the desk over there, folks write their innermost desires of Christmas wishes. Don't underestimate the hearts and giving nature of this town.

"The other box is for deeds when grateful folks who may

have been benefactors on previous occasions want to return goodwill by fulfilling someone else's needs. No one can measure the gifts of charity and fulfillment in helping others."

"I'm at a loss for words," Bradley said. "I've been swept back into childhood fantasy and animation."

"Then we have our vintage North Pole mailbox that the kids come looking for with their letters. My father found that in an antique shop near Lake Champlain. The iron forging under the paint says the Philadelphia Iron Works Company made it in 1898. Can you imagine the history inside this box?"

"Wow. Generations of children used it!"

"Yes, think of the service this old box has provided for hundreds if not thousands of kids. I hope that not many were left disappointed. We pray each year that we can find the resources and intuition to make miracles a reality."

"Is this the parchment?" asked Bradley, lifting a stack of cards in cellophane.

"Yup, they're the ones. We'll take those upstairs with the boxes. Be careful as they are precious and treasures of my Pops. I was meant to follow in his footsteps which is a huge undertaking and honor. Someday, others will carry on, perhaps even my children, but I know the inner calling will find its way to bring the right person."

Rudy raised a finger to his forehead. "I was only thinking aloud; please don't mention to Gary what I said. It will happen if it should in good time and following their desires."

"I understand, Rudy. I will always know that this place is here, and I will try to listen for the calling wherever I go in life."

"To each his own desires, my son."

Rudy eased the boxes from the shelf and caressed and polished them. Bradley received each one as a magnificent honor that he could be part of this ceremony.

"I feel the permeation of the wishes and deeds that these boxes carried over the years. Incredibly, they have changed people's lives."

Rudy stopped to absorb the thought. "Yes, Bradley, that is very true. From time to time, I look back in my ledgers and remember good things that happened.

"Some years ago, a young boy who had leukemia needed a bone marrow transplant, but we couldn't find a suitable match despite all the appeals. He asked his mother to put a wish in our box, and it wasn't more than a few days later, a stranger came into our store and accepted the Deed.

"Unbelievably, he went to the hospital in Stowe to have the test. Incredibly, the doner was the boy's father who had left his family many years before and returned to save his son's life. A few days later, the father and son lay together in a hospital room, reunited."

"That's a painful story with a happy ending. I can't imagine the emotion."

Rudy shook off the feeling and returned to his tasks. "Sadie placed her trestle table in the archway between the Emporium and the café to set up the boxes there. Folks will start coming in to look for them today."

"Who knows they'll be there?"

"Everyone in town, and anyone is encouraged to make a wish or take a deed. Then at the end of the day, the elves step up to make them happen. The process works as a leap of faith by the community and strangers that pass through our doors."

A thought stirred in Bradley's soul. Could *he* dare to put

his heart into print and write out a wish? His desire was simple, but the barrier seemed too great to conquer without help. It had been years since he believed in Santa Claus, but something here was different, with hope and belief.

Surely, others feel as I do, with fractured families needing to find one another.

Rudy saw Bradley's shoulders sag and the worried brow showing a burden in his heart and felt a deep empathy. He knew what needed to happen.

5

Wishes Begin to Fill the Box

Lola Turnbull had given her notice to terminate the
rental agreement on her one-bedroom apartment on
Spruce Drive. Her building was only a few blocks from the
town center, and she knew everyone who had been residents
over the years.

Her decision had been strenuous and complex, but her
doctor and distant family recommended a retirement
residence believing it was time to receive daily medication
and attention. She was becoming forgetful, many times not
eating meals and missing the nutrition she needed.

Her daughter and her husband promised to come to
Chimney Ridge this year to celebrate Christmas with Lola in
her home before the move.

Although the suggestion sounded pleasing, Lola had been
disappointed before and didn't put much faith in that
promise. She knew Diane loved her, but once she had

married and taken a career, the phone calls were seldom, and birthday cards no longer came.

Disheartened that the inevitability of her situation had come, she toyed at sorting things to be donated and given away. Her gnarled fingers pulled at the drawers and hangers, filling bags with usable items for the Salvation Army.

"Aah, look at this, Otis. Remember when I wore this? You were just a wee pup then and wouldn't remember. But look at your tail wag; you like it, don't you?"

Lola swirled before the dressing mirror, seeing the image of a young woman getting ready to dance at the Fezziwig. Then the pain of arthritis interrupted the moment, and the vision disappeared.

She carefully rolled the treasured blue velvet gown into a bag for give-away, joined by the muzzle of Otis, her beloved golden retriever, to help her stuff it in.

She gathered the bags together and resisted a last-minute reconsideration, then gave a deep sigh of resignation. Although she had built an attachment to certain items, and they held memories, now they meant nothing to anyone else. She was exhausted but needed to get out of the mess she had started.

"You're such a good boy, Otis."

The grief was overwhelming, and as tears trickled on her cheeks, the silent nuzzle of his chin landed on her knee. Then it dawned on her that she would need to find him a new loving home.

His brown eyes looked up at her, pleading for her to be content and rub his head. Since coming to her as a stray pup years before, he never left her side and had forced her out for exercise every day.

"My dear, Otis, what am I to do?"

The pooch put his paws on her lap and raised his head to lick her chin. She held his sweet head wishing the pain wouldn't be so great, but she couldn't resist him and lowered her head to rest gently on this soft, warm soul that loved her so much.

"You are a comfort, dear one."

Through the drapes, she could see that the streets had been cleared of the overnight snow. The sun had broken through the morning clouds and was dancing like diamonds on a crisp white blanket.

Lola kissed his head as she struggled with her boots. "Well, my dear, Otis, I have a few errands, but I won't be too long." She gathered her wheeled shopping cart and packed a grocery bag of extras from her kitchen cupboards to drop the goods at the Emporium's food bank box.

Sensing her anguish, he let out a sympathetic whimper.

"Sorry, Otis; I love you, sweetheart."

The retriever stayed at her side until she edged out the door and sighed as he heard the lock.

Lola slowly walked down a flight of stairs to the outside courtyard, lowering the cart at each step. When she took the apartment many years before, it never occurred to her that the stairs would become an obstacle.

Instead, arthritis had overtaken her once brisk pace, and she gripped the cart for support as she strolled in the direction of the main street.

Ahead, she watched the breaks of sunlight filtering through the clouds and looked up at the hands of the town clock. On Saturday mornings, the town always started in slow motion, but today already had more life on the sidewalks.

As Lola walked, her eyes brightened every time she saw a familiar face. First, she passed a foursome of young boys in a snowball fight, then a lad of nine or ten, struggling with the weight of his newspaper bag. She knew Henry Parker was a kind and gentle kid who was always generous when she needed a helping hand.

With the sun in her eyes, she nearly barrelled into the mailman. "Oh, my goodness, I almost didn't see you, Richard; the sun reflecting off the snow is bright for my cataracts. Merry Christmas!" she said as she passed him, slugging his sack of cards and letters.

"Just a minute, Mrs. Turnbull." Richard paused and dug into his bag. "Merry Christmas! I have a small packet for you. I can give it to you now or leave it in your mail slot if you prefer."

Lola replied, wanting any idle chatter. "Kind of you, Richard, but I'm just heading out, and I get forgetful; the mail slot will be fine. You must be busy this time of year."

"I love the season, delivering good wishes and cheer to folks. A crisp, white snowfall puts us all in the mood, right?"

"Yes, it wouldn't be Christmas without snow. Have a nice day!"

Lola hadn't thought of Christmas in that way, as so many spent time alone, waiting for visitors that never came.

In her declining years, Lola lost many friends to illness and old age but forged through tough days helping out at the church and groups whenever she could. Still, she looked for familiar faces to brighten her days.

Henry Parker saw Lola's difficulty pulling her shopping cart through the treads in the snow. As it thawed, the slushy ridges slowed the wheels.

"Mrs. Turnbull, where are you going? I'll give you a hand

as I have a few minutes to spare," the boy scout insisted.

Stopping to catch her breath, she realized she had gotten herself into a predicament with her load against the wet snow furrows. The cart seemed much heavier now.

"That's very generous, Henry; I'm heading for the Emporium. It's just there ahead, but it seems I put more weight into my cart than I realized. It's kind of you to give me a hand."

"Anytime, Mrs. Turnbull. I heard about the parade later; it should be quite the event." Henry said, doing his best at small talk.

"You must be ready for Christmas," said Lola. "What do you want this year?"

"I keep hoping for a bike to help with my newspaper route, but I'd rather new boots for my dad." Henry hung his head with embarrassment.

"What size does your dad wear? My son visited a few years ago and left a fine pair of boots in the closet. They are brand new. Come by and pick them up."

Henry's face lit up. "Are you sure he won't want them?"

"He's long forgotten them. It's a shame for them not to have good use."

"Can I come tomorrow after church?"

Lola smiled as if he'd asked her on a date. "Perfect, I'll have hot chocolate waiting for you."

The clock tower struck nine when Rudy climbed up the basement stairs with two wooden boxes bound for the trestle stand.

"I love this table, Rudy; every year, I see more magic in it," Sadie cooed as she directed the placements on a carved oak pedestal in the main room.

Behind Rudy was Bradley hauling the wrought iron mailbox. He set it on the floor at the top of the stairs to regain his strength and straightened the burlap rug to prevent scratches on the pine floorboards.

"We generally place it close to the door," Rudy said. "The kids can pop in when they are passing by. It's a lovely tradition. Did you see the movie *Miracle on 34th*?"

"I barely remember the story that the Post Office declared Santa Claus was authentic with an obligation to deliver mail addressed to him."

"The Mail Service had the right to deliver letters addressed to the North Pole, proving he exists. A town in Indiana calls itself Santa Claus, and here in Vermont, we take it seriously that all mail for the jolly elf must, in turn, send a reply to each child."

"I never got a letter from Santa in the mail, but when a note was beside my stocking, I was thrilled with that," said Bradley. "But I can envision the thrill for a child to read a letter from Santa."

Sadie handed a green elf hat to Bradley to wear on duty. "Many children ask for new toys," she said, "but most want the gifts of love and assurance. You'll see, Bradley. Perhaps Rudy has that in mind for you."

A small gathering of cheery customers waited outside the Emporium for Rudy to release the latch. As a crush of patrons entered, Bradley's attention turned to the front. "Do I put garland and ribbon on the mailbox? Folks are here already, and the mailbox hasn't been decorated."

"You are right," said Rudy. "That is an essential part of Christmas. Take some fresh boughs and add red and gold baubles from the crate under the table. Make it look enticing for a child. And place a basket of candy canes beside it.

6

North Pole Mailbox

As Bradley dug into his task of arranging the boxes, he let his childish imagination guide him.

In the corner of his eye, he saw a little girl watching him, and her focus didn't leave his face. She wore a red woolen coat with a white rabbit fur collar and earmuffs to match. Her braids were chestnut brown, and her grin boasted two missing teeth.

He melted at her innocence and that she was clutching something in her hand.

"Hello, what's your name?"

She leaned forward and looked quizzically at his apron and sweater.

"Mandy, what's yours?"

Bradley knew this was a momentous moment in Mandy's life, waiting for his reply. She looked beyond his face, into his eyes, his thoughts, and his truth.

"I'm Brad, and I'm here training as an elf. I blew in during the storm last night. I heard that this place is where dreams and wishes come true."

Mandy's eyes filled with wonder as she stared in disbelief. She looked him over and surveyed his height and demeanor.

"I could tell that you are someone special. When you look someone straight in the eye, you can see a bit of their soul, and that's when you know. Do all the elves have blue eyes?"

Looking into her angelic face, he felt something stir in his heart. Something magical. He could see how important the piece of paper she was holding meant to her.

"A lot of us do, in fact, but I have met some very nice elves that have brown eyes. Is that a letter for the North Pole?"

"Yes, this is an *extremely* important letter; will you make sure that Santa receives it in time to fill my wish?"

She neared with her eyes wide to whisper in Bradley's ear. "It's a matter of life and death!"

"That sounds serious," Bradley said, lowering on one knee to be at her height. "You were right to bring your letter to this mailbox for special attention."

A tall woman was meandering nearby and looking back at the transaction between Bradley and Mandy. She couldn't help smiling proudly to herself and waited for Mandy to look up at her for consent.

"You go ahead, Mandy; this is the place," her mother encouraged.

"Here's the mailbox all ready to take your letter," Bradley said. "Just deposit it in the slot, and we'll make sure it gets delivered before Christmas."

He nodded to Mandy's mother, then spoke softly again. "Mandy, when you drop it in, make sure your eyes are closed and listen carefully, then think hard on your wish. After that, you'll hear the gentlest gust of wind sweep it up and send it on its way. I'm sure you've been a good girl this year, and something special will be under your tree."

Mandy's face tightened in sudden distress. "Oh no, it can't go under the tree!"

Bradley reached into his elf apron and drew out a roll of stickers. "Here, I'll put a 'special delivery' notice on your envelope so it will get priority attention."

Mandy inched forward. She closed her eyes, and her head twisted to listen, then she beamed in the satisfaction of the moment.

"I heard it, Mom. I heard the gust of wind." Her eyes sparkled with her bursting imagination.

Rudy's eyes twinkled as he observed their rapport. "Are you going to the festival tonight?" he called to Mandy. "There'll be a parade on main street with sleigh rides, characters marching and on floats, bands, singing, and street dancing. Surely they will have Santa Claus and candy canes."

The child looked up at her mother. "Please, Mom, can we go? Maybe Mr. Jackson would like to come as well. He's been so sad, and it would do him good to see happy things. It might give him hope."

"I suppose," Mrs. Carson said. "Mandy, have a browse around the store while I take a moment with Mr. Hancock to leave the mittens."

At a long slab counter, Mrs. Carson began to remove her collection of knitted mittens for Rudy's approval. "They are fairly standard in size, but we put in a few smaller ones for the younger kids."

"Oh, they're perfect, and the wool is so soft. We've been

waiting for these. I hope you'll have more soon as there's a great demand in town, Mrs. Carson."

She nodded. "That certainly pleases me. I can do about two dozen a week."

"We have visits to seniors' homes, and I have another campaign in mind. Do you think you could recruit some helpers to produce more than the two dozen?"

Mrs. Carson's eyes perked up at the challenge. "I know that I could. I'll go to the craft shop this morning for more wool."

"Maeve will give you a receipt for these, and we'll put them out right away. Come back whenever you have more mittens; they're popular items."

Mandy and her mother left soon after, contented at their morning work.

The shop and the café were both humming with chatter and anticipation. Customers coming and going knew they were entering a sanctuary of Christmas spirit as carols piped through the store on speakers mounted above the shelves. The sights, the sounds, the smells, the whistling and giggling; they were all there.

Clifford Winters could see that it was time for him to leave and make space for someone else. Gathering his coat, he headed for the door. Simultaneously, Lola Turnbull was arriving, with a minor struggle through the door with her shopping cart.

"Good morning, Lola. Let me help you with that."

"Thank you, Cliff; you see, I have a few bags there for the food bank. I'm afraid it has come time for me to give my notice and go to the Pinewoods retirement home." She sighed as she relinquished the handle to Cliff.

"Oh, dear! I can't imagine packing up my home. Since Thelma's been gone, the house is so quiet." Cliff took a moment to think and did his best to offer hope of a more perfect life for his friend. "I know of a few folks who have gone to Pinewoods and found new friends and companionship."

"You look like you're on your way out the door. Would it be too much if I asked you to stay and join me for a cup of coffee? I could use a friendly face and kindly ear."

Clifford suddenly saw Lola differently; it was like magic had cuffed him on the back of the head. She wasn't the little lady with her felt hat and pearl hatpin on Sundays at church; he saw a life of pain and experience in her face and felt a new understanding and connection.

Lola was agile enough to get about town, but she now needed daily medication and nutrition that she could no longer manage on her own.

Prim and proper, she wore a beautiful bouffant of golden-white hair gathered into a French roll with a few wayward wisps that escaped and framed her face. Her eyes sparkled to see his familiar face.

"Of course, Lola, what are friends for?"

7

Deed Remembered

T oward the end of business hours, a distinctive-looking man happened into the Emporium with a woman holding his arm. Carrying himself erect and proper, the man wore handmade, official government polished black boots, and it appeared he was military.

The gentleman's attention went to the short queue of excitable folks filling out wish cards. He was puzzled by the crowd's enthusiasm and curious about the process of the mysterious boxes.

"What are these for?" he asked Rudy. "By the clamor, I can see that everyone is eager, whatever it is."

"It's a long story, but I'll do my best to summarize. It starts with my father, who died twenty years ago. While I was growing up, he said we had everything we needed to be happy—love and family. So there was no need to buy presents for ourselves."

"You had no presents as a child?"

"I'll explain. He taught us it was essential to give to those who couldn't have the joy we shared. My father's philosophy impacted me then, and I watched how he lived his life.

"In the months leading to each holiday season, Pops became interested in the townsfolk and their needs. Whenever he identified desperation, he wrote a gift card and placed it in an envelope on our tree. We each chose one the week before Christmas, and it was incumbent upon us to fulfill that wish."

The man stationed himself with his arms crossed and growing interest. "You did this as children?"

"Yes, they were simple requests from the heart, but enough to change the world for the individual with the request." Rudy had captivated the man's attention, and he nodded toward the commotion at the Wish Boxes.

"How did all of this start then?"

"I have done my best to continue Pops' inspiration for our village to experience joy and the real meaning of Christmas. These folks could be leaving a wish here or picking up a request for a deed, or even dropping off a letter for the North Pole. We get many anonymous requests about needs. Thankfully, there's an abundance of private takers wanting to accept a deed request and fulfill it."

"Is there a recognition for fulfilling one?"

"Oh yes! The reward for doing a deed for someone else is something you never forget."

The man's face softened with intrigue while he looked into Hancock's eyes, and the encounter stirred a fleeting memory.

"Do you remember me, Rudy?"

"Yes, Nate, your dad passed away in town when you were

a boy, and you had to leave your home. Many of your heirlooms went missing. You sent a letter to Santa to ask for the return of your father's war medals as they meant a great deal to your memories of a brave soldier."

Nate's eyes bulged with disbelief.

"How could you know—?"

"As I've heard, sometime later, one of the elves found them in an antique store in Stowe years ago. Didn't you find your dad's medals under your Christmas tree sometime later?"

Nate stepped back to compose himself and his eyes teared up. He tried to talk, but his voice just cracked, and his wife eased up at his elbow to console him. He was astounded to hear Rudy's revelation, and it took him back to the very moment when he saw the medals again.

"Are you alright, dear?"

"Yes, it's wonderful; I'm talking to Santa Claus," he whispered to his wife.

"Incredible, you have no idea what that meant to me, and the medals still do. They sit on my mantle, and I see them every day as a reminder of a great man. It's all that I have of my younger years. I remember that Christmas like yesterday, and whenever of think of my father, I think of that miracle."

"I know he was a brave man. His name has been etched in the Cenotaph monument in the town square. Numerous citizens from Chimney Ridge served in the Second World War and Vietnam, and in other battles where freedom has since been in jeopardy."

"That's true. I understand the reality of war on lives."

"Nate, I've heard that you have a senior military position. With the Iraq-Iran war, your responsibility is great, with lives resting in your hands. Many have lost their lives, hoping to leave an improved world for the next generation. Even though a battle is on foreign soil, everyone is affected at home."

"You're right. Standing here, I'd briefly forgotten the tragedies life holds and how powerless we are to make changes. I still feel pain when a pine box comes back with the American flag, and the hurt is as great as the first time."

"We are never totally powerless, Nate. When you see it, grab that power and make it productive, or it can waste away. You see, I am responsible here for making sure that every request that comes here receives a response. We can each contribute to the spirit of hope and belief no matter what our position."

Rudy noticed that a few patrons had gathered nearby, and he lowered his voice for Nate's ears only. "I know of a little girl who made a seemingly impossible request in her letter to Santa this year. I believe you are just the person to reply to her request. Perhaps you are here for that reason."

"You have an exaggerated idea of my scope of authority in international war. It's flattering, but I think you have misplaced confidence that I could make a change for a child I don't even know. My retirement is in the next year."

The last customer had left the store, and Nate Newman and his wife waited for Rudy's direction as Sadie closed up. Rudy opened the back door of the North Pole box and extracted the letter that was deposited by Mandy earlier that day.

"Take this with you, Nate, and read every word. It is from the simple and pure heart of a young child. It is selfless and reminds us that everyone must believe and have hope. We can make a change happen so someone else's life is better, and we become stronger by doing it.

Nate accepted the envelope with the words 'Santa Claus, North Pole' scribbled in a childish hand. He received it with the honor in which Rudy had given it, knowing that he must fulfill this Deed.

"Thanks for coming today, Nate. You were meant to be here," Rudy said. "Mandy will be at the festival tonight watching for Santa Claus. She already met my new elf, Bradley Rimble, who gave her hope to believe. We are what we allow ourselves to be. If we believe in our hopes and dreams, others will too."

Rudy followed Nate and his wife to the door and watched as they strolled past the Chimney Diner. Large snowflakes were falling gently on the sidewalk under the glow of the Christmas lights and lampposts.

"Come on upstairs for a bite of supper before we go to the parade, Rudy," Sadie called.

"Where's Bradley?"

"I think he's lost in the workshop. It does my heart good to see him come alive and find himself this Christmas."

When the Newmans returned home that night, Nate sat in his favorite armchair and pondered this newfound responsibility that he had accepted. The urgency of Mandy's letter nagged at him, and he unfolded the lined foolscap, pausing to see the childish handwriting.

Dear Santa,

I hope you remember me from my visit to Macy's store in New York. My family went there for Thanksgiving.

You were very kind and asked me what I wanted for Christmas. I said I'd like a Barbie fashion cut-out book, but I've changed my mind.

There's a war across the ocean, and our neighbor, Mr. Jackson, has a son who went to fight for freedom. When Iranians attacked the embassy in Tehran, his oldest son, Barry, was killed. Mr. Jackson's only other son, William, is on the battlefield, and Mr. Jackson fears he will die too.

Please don't bring any presents to my house, just bring Mr. Jackson's only son home for Christmas if you can. I've talked to my brother, Stuey, and sister, Nancy, and they agreed that this is their wish too.

We don't have a chimney, but Mom will leave the front door unlocked. We will leave some cookies and milk for you. Have a safe trip, and thank you for making this change to your list.

Yours truly,
Mandy Carson
94 Chestnut Lane, Hampstead Row, Chimney Ridge

Nate let the letter fall onto his lap and folded his hands over his forehead to embrace the dilemma. This was personal for him now. If he'd received the letter at his office, he would have delegated it to the Home Service unit for a response, but now he had accepted it—a Deed accepted.

He muttered under his breath, "Rudy Hancock, what have you done to me?" He opened his desk to draw out his personal letterhead, and at the top of his drawer was the velvet box that contained his father's war medals.

His hand shook as he reached into the drawer. His memory was vivid of the Christmas when the small, unnoticed box addressed to him was under their tree. His father's absence had been painful, and when he opened the box, he felt a warm flood of the presence of his father and sobbed.

"I can't explain how Hancock was involved, and I don't want to know. I prefer to believe in miracles. Yes, there are miracles, and as the man said, I do have the power to make a change!"

When he finished writing his letter to a friend in Washington at the Department of Defence, he sealed and stamped the letter. Taking a walk to the town center, he went to the post office and deposited his letter in the mail cavity without another thought.

He quietly whispered, "And Admiral Palmer, you do not receive this letter by accident."

A shiver went up Newman's spine, and he looked at the mailbox as if it beheld some magic, like a wisp of stardust had sucked the envelope out and couriered it on its way.

Rudy sat at his kitchen table with Sadie and Bradley, reviewing the day at the Emporium over a bowl of beef stew. He reached for the plate of bread, buttered a thick slice, and cleaned the gravy left in his bowl.

There was no doubt to Rudy that Bradley was embracing his elf position. "You filled your elf shoes well, Bradley."

"My shoes are no different than they were yesterday, but I have dramatically altered my viewpoint."

"What did you see today that is lingering in your heart?"

"So many things. The moment I entered the workshop, I realized the burden of the Wish Boxes. Old Cliff came here only wanting companionship, then Mrs. Turnbull, who was afraid of being alone."

"You're right; they both had needs."

"Then the little girl looked at me as if she genuinely believed I was an elf in training.

"Folks come through the front door looking at one

another, wondering if the others had left wishes or deeds. It's an endearing connection that intertwines them to one another. I'm amazed at this undertaking that you call the spirit of Christmas."

Rudy listened and nodded. "As I said yesterday, you were brought here for a purpose. Sometimes the best way to help yourself is to help others."

Sadie laid a platter in the center of the table. "Speaking of helping yourself, here's a plate of leftover pastries from the bakery."

Bradley was immediately on his feet with the empty bowls. "My mother insisted that we help in the kitchen at home. It's the least I can do here too."

"You must miss your mother, Bradley."

"Yes, I think about my family every day, but I have to be ready to reach out to them. I know that will happen, but pride is a forceful barrier."

"It sometimes holds us back from the right action," said Sadie. "It can happen to anyone."

"Rudy told me I was here for a purpose when I first arrived here, and I've come to believe that. I will finish my elf position first before I make my own plans."

"You are not alone in your experience," said Rudy. "I assure you."

"I was raised to see things through to the best of my ability when accepting responsibility. You can always rely on me."

"One night, we'll go to the mission to serve in the kitchen. You'll see other young people in similar situations feeling as you do with their own stories and secrets. But some others are less fortunate without good memories."

"The snow is starting, and we should get ready for the

parade," said Sadie. "I always prepare a large pot of hot chocolate on a cold night as a handful of folks will linger afterward."

"Use the warm down coat on the rack in the downstairs hall and a colorful felt toque," said Rudy. "You must appear elfish, remember."

8

The First of December Parade

Well before seven, the sidewalks were already alive with families and tourists who had flooded in for the event. At seven-ten, the strains of a marching band echoed from the town courtyard centered by the clock tower.

Leading in front, a line of drums and a chorus of brass instruments by a motley group of juniors from the high school marched proudly in precision onto the street.

The church organized the first float with a stable of rustic barn wood and straw, characterizing Mary, Joseph, and the baby in a manger.

Next was a small herd of roaming sheep led by a shepherd and a pair of round-up collies that kept the route orderly, fascinating the children on the curb. Kennedy Farms suited up a couple of donkeys and a few llamas for amusement.

Lagging were two stilted performers in paper-mache masks in the likeness of Mr. and Mrs. Fezziwig. Running to and fro in the forefront, a class of tiny children danced their Irish jigs.

The high school built a float of the North Pole workshop with kindergartners tossing candy canes, tooting on kazoos, and twirling batons to keep them warm. An open-stake truck with mountains of hay bales carried 4H club members cradling baby lambs.

Three merchants outfitted as kings with robes and golden crowns strolled behind, followed by teens leading costumed dogs in all breeds and sizes, bringing laughter up and down the street.

"Ho, Ho, Ho," the mayor shouted as he waved from the rumble seat of a flag-draped antique, with a wreath harnessed to the front grill.

The new addition was the town's brand-new fire truck with its dalmatian mascot. As clusters of children called to hear the new siren, the Captain let it roar on every block.

The finale was a sleigh, escorted by children's voices of 'Here Comes Santa Claus,' with Santa standing tall, waving and calling names of boys and girls over a megaphone.

Bradley spotted Mandy Carson with her mother. Her bubbly personality showed from ear to ear as she balanced on tiptoes, waving frantically to be seen by the jolly red elf. He made his way through the crowd and hoisted her onto his shoulders. "There, Mandy, can you see now?"

"Yes, that is better, and I've straightened your hat. Santa will see me, I know because I'm with one of his elves."

Bradley winked at Mrs. Carson.

Traditionally, Rudy's Emporium opened an hour after the parade passed for folks to warm up, and Sadie's urn of cocoa and platters of gingerbread cookies were ready for the children.

Clifford Winters waited outside to help with the after-parade crush. When he caught Sadie's eye, she opened it for him, and he immediately went to the café to pour the hot drink into take-out cups.

"Other years, you know Thelma would lend a helping hand," he said, "so I'm just carrying on the tradition."

"Well then, if you want to continue it, you'll have to learn to bake," she urged.

"That would make me more useful. I always helped Thelma with her Christmas cake, mostly chopping, though. I'll dig out her recipes and give it a go sometime."

"Instead, Cliff, why don't you show up tomorrow morning at about six and help me with the café baking. I know you're an early riser. We used up everything we had for today, and it's quite a chore for one person."

"I can do that, and I know someone else who might like to be needed in some way."

"Who's that?"

"Lola Turnbull."

"Yes, I saw her come into the shop today but didn't get to visit. She will be moving to Pinewoods after Christmas. When you've lived in one place for a long time, it's hard to pull up roots and start over with a different environment and new faces. Poor dear won't like that much."

"Why do you say that?" Cliff asked.

"Lola had slowed down with arthritis," said Sadie. "She may not take time to make three meals a day, but her mind is sharp as a whip."

"Pinewoods?" Cliff repeated. "There are many folks with dementia and other handicaps at Pinewoods."

"It's too early for Lola; I still see her most days walking

on the main street. It's too bad she doesn't have a family to take her in. Loneliness could be the biggest part of her decline."

Cliff was quiet, suddenly embarrassed about how little he knew about his long-time friend.

"Weren't Lola and Thelma good friends?" Sadie asked.

"Yes, they were. Lola helped to brighten the days when Thelma fell ill. I'd forgotten how much we enjoyed her companionship. Once Thelma passed, it seemed awkward for her to come by for a visit. I guess I could have been a more helpful friend."

"It's a reminder of how important companionship is to each of us, especially as we enter the twilight years. Lola has lived in town her whole life. All she has now is Otis."

"Otis?"

"Her beloved golden retriever. It will break her heart to have to give him up. He's been good for her, and it will leave a big void. She's rather worried about finding a new forever home for him."

"Of course, I do remember Otis. A nice boy he is. I always wanted a dog, but Thelma had allergies, and I stopped thinking about it."

Sadie understood Lola's situation all too well and deliberately planted the seed of interest with Cliff Winters.

Why should two lonely people and a devoted dog not find each other at Christmas?

The following weekend would be the seniors' residence visit, and Pinewoods was on the Hancocks' list. Sadie planned on a personal box of baked goodies for each person, hand-knit mittens from the Ladies Auxiliary, a collectible gift from the Emporium, and the traditional candy cane.

"Rudy, you could recruit Cliff to join us on Saturday's

Pinewoods tour. He could bring Lola along, and perhaps she will see the manor in a more positive light." Sadie's wink told him she had an entirely different angle in mind.

"That shouldn't be a problem as Cliff gets attached to us at Christmas; besides, I already proposed to him the thought of fitting into the Santa suit."

Across town, Lola Turnbull was sipping a cup of tea in her kitchen with Otis's soft head on her knee. She examined the parcel Richard left in her mail slot and nodded, recognizing her daughter's return address in New York.

She unwrapped a book on *Aging Gracefully* and a delicate bottle of rosewater from Woolworths and appreciated their thoughtfulness.

There was no card, but gathering up the paper, she noticed a small slip of paper, merely a note. She had received these letters in the past instead of the courage of a phone call. Every time, her heart sank with the pain of rejection and disappointment. Something had come up, and they wouldn't be coming for Christmas after all.

"I can't say we didn't expect this, Otis."

She rubbed the soft head on her knee, and his brown eyes looked up at her with more love than she could ask for.

"Well, Otis, my darling, we can't sit here feeling sorry for ourselves. I still have some Christmas decorations packed away; let's get them out for the last time and put on some lively music."

The dog's head popped up, and he sprang up with his tail wagging, eager to help.

Looking longingly at the senior pup, she pondered that perhaps she could inquire of Rudy Hancock or place a request in the Christmas Deed Box.

"Loving, loyal dog needs a good forever home after Christmas. He is extra special and devoted, loves children and cuddles. That's what my note will say."

Lola unpacked two cardboard boxes from her closet and set out a pre-lit artificial pine tree and a few of her lifetime treasures and decorations.

A side table with open shelves held her vintage record albums, and she thumbed through each LP associating memories.

She placed her favorite on the turntable, 'I Yust go Nuts at Christmas' by Yogi Yorgesson, and turned the volume up high, so it filled the room. Next was 'Yingle Bells', and she twirled by the window as she mimicked and sang along.

"Otis, do you remember how the children used to laugh when we played these? Let's do 'Jive Bunny' next; they loved that one. None of those sad, make-us-cry tunes like 'I'll Be Home for Christmas.' "

The brown eyes perked up, and he pranced his front paws on the floor in excitement.

"That's my boy."

Despite the lively music and the tree lights and decorations, Lola had a tear of sadness and deep loneliness in her eye.

She remembered the conversation earlier with young Henry Parker, and from the back corner of the hall closet, she pulled out a box, a pair of new brown leather winter thermal boots she'd purchased for her son. She remembered the laborious decision to buy them, convinced by the stock clerk in Stowe that it was the latest trend.

Believing her son would be thrilled with the efforts, she looked forward to him opening it that Christmas, three years ago.

Her son and his wife arrived on their way to New York and took Lola out for dinner. They talked about friends, social obligations, and contributions to their church but expressed no curiosity about her life in Chimney Ridge.

They didn't ask how she was doing, how she filled her days, or if she needed anything. Their lives had become busy, and she had come to wonder if they were interested in hers.

She invited them back to her apartment for tea, and while it was still hot, they rose to depart. She tried to persuade them to open a pair of presents, the expensive winter boots for Davis, and a hand-knit sweater made with love for Diane.

"Merry Christmas, Mom, but we have to go. Call you later." They were out the door, and that was the last Lola saw of them in the three long years since.

"Do you remember that, Otis?" He turned his head, trying to understand.

"I showed Davis the boots, but he didn't seem to notice, and left them in the box. He's never asked for them in three years."

She placed them on the table, satisfied that Henry would come on Sunday.

9

Plans Laid for Fezziwig

Rudy's phone rang late in the evening, and he was right in predicting it was Mrs. Middleton from the Fezziwig Organizing Committee, as she had no hesitation in calling him day or night in the interest of the ball.

Her committee of six members and a host of volunteers had achieved recognition for their roles in the annual festive ball touted throughout Vermont. It was regarded as prestigious to be part of the Fezziwig, and Mrs. Middleton took full advantage of that status.

"Rudy, it's a catastrophe! We need an emergency meeting for the morning."

"Can you give me a heads up, Myrtle?"

"I'm afraid the band that we contracted from Albany has just canceled and returned our deposit. The ball is only two weeks away, and I don't know what we can do on short notice. Everyone in town looks forward to this event, and

I'll be a laughingstock if this isn't fixed! It's the Fezziwig! We can't have Christmas in Chimney Ridge without it."

Rudy used a soothing voice to calm Mrs. Middleton. "Don't worry, Myrtle, I'll do some research and check the leads I might have. I promise you that I will find a replacement. We'll talk in the morning."

"Yes, Rudy, you're right. Perhaps I am overreacting."

Although it was late, Rudy called an old friend in Concord who recommended a band, and curiously the organizer's name tweaked his interest. He called right away, and as soon as the voice spoke, Rudy knew he'd found the right person.

"First of all, do you know who Fezziwig is?" Rudy asked.

The man on the phone cackled with laughter. "Of course, I know about Fezziwig; our family loves Christmas. I assume you want lively music. For jigs, we have some good fiddlers, a banjo player, a violinist, bass guitar, and we can supplement with a brass ensemble."

Satisfied that the substitution would suit the committee, Rudy placed two matching stick pins for Chimney Ridge and Concord on the map in the workshop.

"Another task is completed, and what a miraculous coincidence!"

Late into the night, Rudy worked in the basement workshop. It was only the first day of offering the Deeds and Wish Boxes, yet the early success overjoyed Rudy.

The table's center had separate piles of wish cards, special requests for deeds, and heartfelt letters to Santa Claus.

Rudy sorted the cards into stacks for follow-up. Lola Turnbull signed the first one he picked up: a new bicycle for Henry Parker to do his newspaper route.

The next was anonymous: 'Sandra Davidson wants to be

an Olympic skater like Dorothy Hamill but doesn't have figure skates.' Another said, 'Valerie Metcalfe wants to learn to play the piano like her grandmother used to.'

As he patiently attended to each one, he placed another stickpin on his map.

Most of the letters to Santa Claus could be resolved quickly, but a few would require more work to ensure the child received their request in time for Christmas.

He followed up with the Santa letter, placing a marker for Nate Newman and Mandy Carson in town. Two more for Clifford Winters and another for Lola Turnbull, who had secretly left anonymous wishes for others in the box. Rudy had known Clifford all his life while he lived in the house behind the hardware store. However, he could see a void without Thelma and that he longed for friendship and a life companion.

Lola's wish was two-fold; she didn't want to enter the retirement facility and was heartbroken to leave dear Otis behind. She needed to find him a home, and all the rest would be bearable.

"Those will take some work, but the plan is underway. Sadie is orchestrating that." Rudy's eyes flitted back and forth mischievously at the impending scheme. "My dear Sadie cannot pass on the challenge of match-making."

The raft of wish cards far exceeded the reduction of deed cards he was removing.

"I'll have to talk to the Reverend."

Rudy met with Mrs. Middleton at nine on Monday morning about entertainment for the Fezziwig Ball. She had seconded a rudimentary office in the basement of the Community Center that sufficed for the purpose. He found her stewing over details but expressed his enthusiasm, hoping to satisfy her.

"I managed to speak to a few people last evening, and I found a fellow in Concord that comes recommended. The group has fiddlers and brass instruments and will work well with the pace of the ball, with lots of jive."

"Sort of Bluegrass, you're saying, right? Do they understand what the Fezziwig is?"

"Yes, they assured me of that."

"Will they agree to our fee, though?" she asked.

"Yes, they only ask for a hot meal and gas money for their bus, but they are donating the actual fee back to our homeless shelter."

"We don't exactly have a homeless shelter . . . other than your place," Mrs. Middleton teased, realizing the irony of her comment. "I've heard that you've taken in another drifter for the holidays."

"Yes, Bradley is familiar with the mission soup kitchen, and the church sets up cots in their basement on cold nights. He's a good worker, and we're glad to have him. Both of these efforts for the homeless can take advantage of the contribution from the band."

"Does the group have a name?"

"Finding Fathers! That's their name. Many of the band members are searching for missing children. This allows them to circulate in other communities for sons and daughters that may be homeless. They only perform on weekends as most are regular working folks with day jobs."

"You've got my vote, Rudy. I suggest we confirm it before we lose this band too. The church ladies will provide a hot meal for them before the dance, and we'll pay for their gas from the ticket revenue."

Rudy's eyes were racing. "I'm glad we have that resolved; this time of year, I am calling in all my favors."

"Is there something else I can do for you?"

"Yes, I'm sure there is something, Myrtle, but with only three wishes from the Christmas genie, I have to consider them carefully to make the best use. Can I let you know?"

"Of course, Rudy, anytime. I'll rally my troops to create excitement and gossip to enlist more event volunteers."

Although matronly in appearance, Myrtle was spunky. She giggled with enthusiasm and kicked up her feet in a dance step. "I'll stop by the Emporium later for the band's details."

Rudy's busy agenda took him directly to find Reverend Atkins in his office at the old Baptist Church on Slater Street. It was a short walk from the Post Office, and the lights were already burning in the pastor's office. He mounted the cement stairs and swung one of the great double doors open to the sounds of choir practice filling the sanctuary.

The sopranos were singing 'O Come All Ye Faithful,' and Rudy thought of his mother, who had once belonged to that same group. He soaked in the recollection and locked out the world for this moment.

"Ah, every child who has a mother remembers her singing voice."

In the moment's enjoyment, he didn't hear the Reverend behind him.

"Pleasant morning, Rudy!" How can I help you?"

"Hello, Reverend, yes indeed. Can I have a word with you?"

"Of course, Rudy, anytime. Come into my office. With Christmas on the horizon, I was expecting your visit. We generally make announcements about the Wish and Deeds program in our service, considering it part of our outreach. It's always important to be charitable, and especially at Christmas."

The Reverend was a large man with a handlebar mustache and thinning dark hair swept over the top of his head. He had never married and was slightly portly and obliged many parishioners with his acceptance of Sunday dinner invitations. He was blessed with a booming voice that served him well during his Sunday sermons.

"You're right; it's come time for the Wish and Deeds boxes at the Emporium. I'd appreciate your appeal to the benevolent nature of your Sunday congregation to search their hearts in earnest to do a good deed. We've only had the display out for a few days, and already the wishes far exceed the interest in taking deeds to fulfill."

"Ah, yes, every year, we need a little reminding."

Atkins sighed his contentment and leaned back in his chair. "Our town has a big heart, and we'd be failing our neighborhood if we didn't pick up the slack for those in need. Do you want volunteers?"

"We need Christmas spirit, in the principle that it's better to give than receive. Our country is facing battle in Iraq, and here at home, we have unemployed, shut-ins, forgotten seniors, single mothers struggling to provide Christmas for little ones, those facing declining health, and some with broken hearts."

"I think you've covered most needs right there, Rudy."

"Although the community provides for food banks, soup kitchen, carol singing at retirement homes, and meal delivery to the sick and shut-ins, it's deeper than that."

"Do you have a specific suggestion, Rudy?"

"Most activities are already planned, but we could do more here in the same spirit. For example, we could ask your volunteers to add specific decorations to the tree in your sanctuary before the nativity pageant."

The Reverend let it sink in. "Do you mean you'd decorate the tree with needs?"

"The wise men bear gifts, so it fits the theme. It's close enough to Christmas to collect the Wishes and Deeds and allow participants to fulfill the requests. I've heard of this type of effort, and folks referred to it as the giving tree. But Pops told me as a kid that it was the 'living' tree."

"What kind of deeds should we expect?"

"Many are basic human kindness; a young boy is suffering from kidney failure needing a donor, others have empty places at the table where a loved one is no longer there. A businessman without a family has no one to share a Christmas dinner.

"We cannot overlook those that don't complain then go unnoticed; we are not that kind of town. As every year, there are requests for skates, sleds, bikes, and pups. These are deep-seated desires and quite simple if you find the right person to comply."

"You've thought this through, Rudy."

"Well, yes. Mrs. Carson could head up a knitting group for Christmas mittens. We could place a wish or deed in each pair and hang them on the tree with color codes for various categories. The parishioners that wish to participate can select a pair of mittens and will assume responsibility to see that it is fulfilled before Christmas Eve."

Reverend Atkins pondered the scenario, scratched his chin, then leaned forward onto his elbows, moved at the effort of locals toward the town.

For a moment, Rudy wondered if he'd fallen asleep, but it occurred that the Reverend was taking a moment for prayer. Suddenly, Atkins' head jerked, and he looked dazzled.

"If you are certain that will work, I'll put it into my Sunday sermon. Of course, you'll need to keep tabs on the mittens and requests to be sure that no one gets overlooked." Atkins leaned back, satisfied.

"My family and I will take responsibility for any that are left. No one will have a request unfilled, I assure you, Reverend. I have a helper this year, Bradley Rimble. I'll introduce him to you and let him oversee the arrangements."

"Excellent, I'll look forward to meeting Bradley."

Instead of returning to the Emporium, Rudy hurried to the Towne Wool shop. With bags filled with supplies, he headed to Chestnut Lane to find Mrs. Carson to relay his news.

"One way or another, the mitts will be ready. If I need Sadie to teach Bradley to knit in his sleep, so be it."

Rudy chortled with his deepening mischief.

10

Santa Mail Delivered to Washington

At the Pentagon in Arlington, Virginia, Monday's early mail was arriving. The postal van passed through security clearance at the gated government stone edifice and parked in its usual drop-off area.

A Special Delivery cardboard envelope separated from the regular mail containers was taken immediately to the Department of Defence, requiring a signature from General Preston Watson.

Watson, a tall, broad-shouldered man in uniform, passed by the reception desk as the envelope arrived. The delivery clerk recognized the General and glanced at the ID on his uniform. He wasn't sure if he was required to salute, then made a half-hearted effort to be sure.

"Excuse me, General Watson, Sir, an envelope here requires your signature."

Watson grunted and signed, snatching the mail. He read

the return address and tucked it under his arm.

"I can't say that I'm expecting anything from Vermont that would require my immediate attention, however—."

"Thank you, sir, and Merry Christmas."

The clerk offered a hap-hazard salute for the inconvenience and interruption. Watson scowled at the incompetence and walked. "That lad should be enlisted and taught appropriate respect," he muttered.

Watson continued to his office and tossed the delivery pouch to a corner tray. But as he read through his daily schedule, his eyes kept wandering back, and he picked it up again. He thought he recognized the sender's name.

"Chimney Ridge! Where is that? It sounds like a row of chimneys. Ah, Nate Newman, it's been a while. I wonder what's so dang important that he has to find me here. Doesn't he know there's a war going on?"

Slitting the flap, he removed Nate's letter, and the enclosure fell onto his desk. He flipped it over. "What's this mean? It's addressed to Santa Claus, North Pole."

Nate had been to the point. Wishing the family health and happiness over the holidays, he was burdened to send the little girl's wish from Chimney Ridge, Vermont.

The selfless wish of this young girl was handed to me, and I am obligated to perform the impossible deed. You see, her heart is heavy with the anguish of her neighbor, a retired military veteran, who lost his oldest son, Barry Vincent Jackson, this time last year. He has one other son who is presently on the front lines in Iraq and in similar danger.

The child pines daily, watching Mr. Jackson's anguish as if the notification unit could again arrive at his door. All he would want is to see his son William for Christmas.

I understand we have taken oaths to protect freedom and democracy and defend the value of lives at home and in foreign countries. However, I have seen the pain brought to parents who lost a child. One alone is too much, and to leave the last son in the line of fire may fall under compassion. Does it deserve the power of intervention by those who have the authority? Is there room here to invoke the sole survivor rule?"

The letter continued with the recitation of pledges of allegiance, but Watson quickly glazed over it. He sat back in his chair and glanced at a photograph on his desk of his wife, ten-year-old daughter, and two teenage sons who would be eligible for enlistment in a few years.

The hard lump in his throat would not ease, and he picked up the childish writing addressed to Santa Claus.

Please don't bring any presents to my house, just bring Mr. Jackson's son home.

General Watson was aware that his own family was together, safe at home, planning a day of Christmas shopping and evening festivities with relatives.

He knew that so many of his friends and neighbors were oblivious to what was happening in the world of war, yet today's fatalities and front-line status reports lay on the desk for his attention.

A Lieutenant rapped at his door and reminded him of a meeting in the conference room. Watson turned away from the letter and soon became involved in other matters throughout the day.

In the evening, driving up to his house, he thought more about his family's comfort. The entire trim of the home was lit up with hundreds of colored bulbs that glowed to the street, and the living room window curtains were drawn back to display an enormous pine tree ladened with decorations.

"When you are blessed, it's easy to overlook others who do not have so much."

After supper, he tucked in his own little Emmeline that he assumed must be the same age as Mandy Carson. Her blue eyes looked up at him adoringly and with innocence as he brushed away a lock of curls that draped over her brow.

"Good night, darling!"

"Daddy, what do you want for Christmas this year?"

"I have everything I want right here in this house. A present doesn't have to be wrapped and under the tree. It can be something you've made, like a drawing, a card, a painted rock, or anything that you've given thought about to make another person smile."

The little girl believed her father would solve her worries. "Does Santa go to war at Christmas? Does everyone come home for Christmas? What about all those people far away? Do they get Christmas too?"

"Christmas comes every year, and so does Santa. He gets to every house around the world. Have sweet dreams now, Emmeline."

"Hmph, probably both of them are missing their two front teeth." He mused as he closed the bedroom door behind.

Watson was awakened repeatedly through the night by the nagging that William Jackson's life was in his hands. It was particularly poignant at Christmas.

"Here I am, bearing the responsibility for another man's son on the anniversary of the death of a family member."

He glanced at the clock. "I wonder where William Jackson is at this moment. He might be under attack now." The clock ticked louder.

He thought of his sons and daughter and the loss of his father as a soldier, leaving a painful empty feeling that remained. He recalled the many times he saluted a coffin arriving back in America after the ultimate sacrifice.

"I fear that I could be too late. But every moment counts; we only have so many in our lives."

In the morning, General Watson walked briskly and with determination into the Pentagon, inherently aware of the power in the hands of the few.

"Maxwell! A file is on my desk for Private William Jackson. Please get the paperwork going for a compassionate discharge as soon as possible. He is serving in the hot zone in Khorramshahr and must be home for Christmas. He is a sole survivor."

Five days later, as Nate Newman was receiving a reply from General Watson, little Mandy Carson was watching through her window for the morning mail.

When a camouflaged military jeep stopped at Mr. Jackson's Chestnut Lane house, he was brushing snow from the sidewalk, a change from his morning routine of rocking on the veranda, watching neighborhood life.

Mandy shrieked at first sight of the jeep, suspecting bad news. Her heart sank, and she watched Mr. Jackson as he stood at attention, trembling, unsure of what was happening.

A young private hopped out of the back, tossed his gunny sack to the road, and stood at the end of his father's gate in a salute.

"William," the old veteran called in an unbelieving

whisper. "Is it really you?"

"It's me, Pop; it looks like Santa wanted me home for Christmas this year." The young man's gaunt face grinned from ear to ear.

Mandy stayed straining through the window over the back of her living room couch, watching the joyful embrace of father and son. At this moment, she knew in her heart that Santa was real, and her wish was fulfilled.

"He really did get my letter!"

11

Anticipation in the Emporium Queue

Bounding back down the main street, Rudy was tickled to see a lineup of patrons waiting to enter the Emporium. He nodded to a plump woman standing by the front with others from the horticultural club.

"Hello, Helen, nice to see you this fine morning."

"Good day, Rudy; we've been outside for ten minutes. Will someone ever come out? Surely there is room inside for a few more."

As the door sprung open, out came Carole Davenport ladened with parcels. The aroma of Christmas and the sound of cheerful chatter and gaiety wafted through the doorway to the sidewalk crowd.

Rudy spotted his senior elf through the open door. "Micah, see that these lovely folks get a tasting of Sadie's warm apple strudel while they wait for their turns."

The disgruntled horticultural club sighed in unison and

relaxed their tension, realizing they'd become special. They didn't want Rudy to know that an essential part of the Emporium adventure was waiting in the line outside. It was a chance to catch up on delicious town gossip, see what folks were buying, and hear who would be in town for the holidays.

The baritone from the barbershop quartet appeared minutes later with a basket with tissue and bows, and to the group's pleasure, he sang his version of 'These are a few of my Favorite Things.'

"Alright, folks, think of your own favorite things," said Micah as he passed out strudel samples from his tray.

"I am sure our shelves are brimming with all that you want. But I remind you that the Christmas spirit is required by all those that pass through these doors. If you need assistance, ask anyone in a green elf hat; and if you can't think of anything to buy for yourself or a friend, remember our Deed Box that will bring a reward to your heart."

Micah retreated into the store then turned back. "If children of any age want a demonstration on our marionette puppets, we have a lad that will show you."

Outside, the chitchat carried on with stories of Wishes and Deeds over the years.

Helen declared, "I remember when young Benedict Thompson . . . you all remember Benedict, the lad in the church who now plays the violin so beautifully. He was so enamored when he heard a Bach concerto on the radio that he begged his mother for lessons, but sadly, they were unable to provide them."

"Ah, yes, Benedict, he was a determined lad," Eleanor Partridge interrupted. "Then Mr. Clarkson, an orchestra conductor from Stowe, came one time and asked him to try out *his* violin in the church basement. He was quite impressed and told Mrs. Thompson that her son had talent."

Helen jumped back in. "He said the boy might have the potential for a future career, maybe even at Carnegie Hall. Then, that very Christmas, guess what Benny received from Santa Claus?"

"I think it was the conductor from Stowe that sent it," Eleanor surmised, to the amusement of everyone who had gathered tighter for the tales.

Another voice chimed up from behind. "I can speak from personal experience. Two years ago, my husband was injured on the job, and the season was bleak for our children. I was disheartened and dreading Christmas morning, but there was a light knock at the door at about ten o'clock on Christmas Eve."

"Who was there?" Helen pressed quickly. "Who was at the door?"

"By the time I got my robe on, no one was waiting, but instead, there were boxes of wrapped gifts and food. I was awe-struck that the presents for each of my children were exactly what they had asked for in their Santa letters."

"It's hard to know for sure, it could have come about through rumor, or someone took the request from Rudy's Deed Box. We're not supposed to know the ins and outs of Wishes and Deeds," said Eleanor. "We can make requests for others that are too proud to do it for themselves; then whenever we are able, we should select a deed. I took one last year, and I was surprised that it hardly cost me anything; it wasn't a tangible gift but was something from the heart to show caring."

A man back in the line enjoyed listening to the women go on and hoped that Eleanor might elaborate on the deed she performed. He moved forward so he wouldn't be excluded from the conversation. The tourist was here waiting strictly by accident, asking at his hotel about a good place for Christmas shopping near Stowe. A short time later, he found himself enamored with the quaint town of Chimney Ridge.

The doorbell jangled once more as two ladies departed. Bradley was at the door to welcome the next in line. "Room for two more, please!"

Helen scrutinized the lad wearing the elf hat and voiced her approval for others to hear. "Ah, so you are the new elf that Rudy found for this year."

"Yes, Ma'am, it's an awesome place to be at Christmas. I hope you enjoy your visit to the Emporium. If there's anything you can't find, I'd be more than happy to help."

"What's your name? Your face is familiar; perhaps I've seen you around town before," Eleanor asked.

Ushering the two ladies in, he turned back with a fistful of flyers in hand. "It won't be too much longer, and we thank all of you for your patience. I'll pass out flyers of this week's specials if you're interested."

Philip Grayber accepted the leaflet as he moved up in the line, enthralled in the small-town talk. He wasn't a tall man but was wiry and agile, nondescript, and hardly noticeable in a woolen cap and a neck scarf. It was easy to blend into obscurity and be absorbed into the residents' gossip without question.

His enthusiasm rose as the queue shared tales about the mystique that befell Chimney Ridge every Christmas. A shiver ran up his spine as if he were cast in an imaginary scene.

Opening one of Rudy's flyers, he read about the Emporium's Wishes and Deeds and the town's extensive calendar for the festive season. A surge of passion overwhelmed him. "I must participate in this!"

The chalets and lodges were already booked with skiers and vacationers drawn to the fresh powder snow. Families were bundling into cars destined for Stowe, returning for hiking trails, skiing, ziplining, gondola rides, Ben & Jerry's ice cream factory tours, and breweries.

As snowflakes fell, the lampposts and colored lights created an idyllic environment for Christmas shopping in the antique and craft shops.

Grayber was one of those who rebooked for Stowe every year.

Cyril Metcalf, a local attorney, was waiting outside the Emporium with his wife and young daughter when Clifford Winters arrived.

"Good morning, Cliff; nice to see you on this snowy morning."

"Yes, 'tis a fine morning. I felt sorry for myself these past months with my wife gone, but this week I've been pitching in with Rudy and Sadie, and I must say it's done my heart good."

"It brings everyone together," added Mrs. Metcalf. "You know, in all the years I've been coming to the Emporium and enjoying the town's events, I've never heard anyone complain or argue."

"I didn't see Lola Turnbull at church yesterday. Do you know how she's doing?" Cyril asked.

"Lola is a fine lady," said Clifford. "We had coffee the other day. Unfortunately, she is preparing for the retirement residence across town. I'll miss her smile, as she called Thelma every day, and we always knew that she would come whenever we asked." Clifford's thoughts drifted for a moment. "She really is a special person."

"I heard that rumor at choir practice this week. Poor dear, I can't imagine the strain of leaving her home and everyone she knows and moving to a strange place," said Mrs. Metcalf. "She lived her whole life in this community and raised her children here. She has arthritis but is still spry and has a thriving spirit."

"Yes, I hadn't thought of it that way. There must be another way for Lola. I'd miss her for certain; she was a big part of my life over the years." Clifford found himself visualizing Lola's face, sparkling eyes, and porcelain skin with a hint of rouge and with her white bouffant twisted over her head. His vision was of a dear and beautiful friend, and he realized how much he'd come to rely on her.

Mrs. Metcalf wasn't one to hold her tongue when it came to matchmaking. "Perhaps, you could bring Lola with you for dinner at our place one night this week. We can catch up as old friends do."

Clifford was surprised to hear himself eagerly accept the invitation and planned how he'd suggest it to Lola.

Valerie Metcalf was tugging at her mother's coat. "Mom, you're so busy talking, it's time to move up in the line. I can't wait for our turn to see the marionettes. Look, Mrs. Hancock is putting a Fezziwig in the window, full of ruffles and bustles. It's just magnificent!" The child moved closer to press her nose against the window to see better.

The gaggle outside was captivated and hushed by the commotion in the front window. Bradley and Micah were placing a life-size mannequin dressed in abundant frills and brocades among a troupe of dancing pirouettes. Fishing line wires were manipulating the movements to the fascination of onlookers.

Mr. Grayber was spell-bound but was befuddled about the mention of Fezziwig. He turned around to face the Metcalf's a few patrons behind.

"Excuse me, but may I ask what a Fezziwig is? I'm staying near Stowe and heard about this town, and I couldn't resist my curiosity; it sounds like an enchanting place to be at Christmas."

"Well, then, welcome to Chimney Ridge. It's the culmination of the manger in Bethlehem, the shepherds, Fezziwig, Santa Claus, and the elves workshop all in one. But you are right to ask about the Fezziwig. In two weeks, we will all gather at the community center, all dressed in period costumes. You've seen the Scrooge movie, of course?"

"Scrooge, yes," Grayber realized. "Ah, I seem to remember now about a gregarious gathering, dancing, and feasting. It emphasized the contrast between Ebenezer, the miser, and the generous flamboyance of goodwill."

"It's the only Fezziwig Ball that I know of. You can get tickets here at the Emporium or the town hall. It's an experience you'll remember for a lifetime," Mrs. Metcalf said.

"Thank you, Mrs—."

"Metcalf, and you are?"

"Philip Grayber. I appreciate the information. Listening to the townsfolk has invigorated my belief in Santa."

Tiny Valerie Metcalf burst into the conversation. "Santa! Of course, there's a Santa."

Grayber looked at the young girl who was searching his eyes for a glimmer of belief.

"Have you visited Santa this year, young lady?" Grayber asked.

"Not yet, but my friend Mandy Carson sent a letter, right here in the post box that goes to the North Pole. It's a secret what she asked for, but I know for a fact that her wish came true!"

"That's awesome. There's a mailbox right here that goes to the North Pole?"

"Oh, yes, it's an extraordinary one you'll see. It's as old as Santa himself. You'll see it says so; the Philadelphia Iron Works made it more than a hundred years ago."

Just then, Rudy reappeared to assess the window display from outside. Coatless, in a red cardigan and carpenter's apron, his arms crossed over his plump chest, and his white curls were awry.

Valerie couldn't help but giggle, and she whispered to Grayber. "See, there he is!"

"What do you folks think of Sadie's window?" Rudy called out to the crowd.

"Every year, it's even better. It's delectable, Rudy!" Mrs. Metcalf confirmed over murmurs of approval.

12

Patta-patta-pan, Turra-lurra-lay

Micah ushered another group into the store as an orderly handful of shoppers left in excited chatter. As Grayber pushed in, he was accosted by a cluster of elves announcing a translated French carol they were about to sing.

"It's called *Patapan*, by Patrick de La Monnoye from the 1700s," said Micah. "Listen carefully to the mimic of the drums in the patta-pan and the flute in the turra-lurra-lay."

One blew into a wooden instrument to start the melodic voices of the elves.

Billy, bring your new red drum,
Robby, get your fife and come
Fife and drum together play,
Patta-patta-pan, turra-lurra-lay,
Fife and drum together play,
On this joyous Holiday

When the men of olden days
To the King of Kings gave praise,
On the fife and drum did play,
Patta-patta-pan, turra-lurra-lay,
On the fife and drum did play,
So their hearts were glad and gay

There is music in the air
You can hear it everywhere,
Fife and drum together play,
Patta-patta-pan, turra-lurra-lay,
Fife and drum together play,
On this joyous Holiday

God and man today become
More in tune than fife and drum,
Fife and drum together play,
Patta-patta-pan, turra-lurra-lay,
Fife and drum together play,
On this joyous Holiday.

Bradley was prominent in his green beret and a toy drum hanging from a lanyard. Beside him, Micah whistled on a toy flute as if he were the Pied Piper. Together, the line of elves kicked up their knees and feet in rhythm. Within minutes, the children were clambering for toy drums and flutes.

To Rudy, it was the sound of euphoria and happiness. He stretched over the heads for Sadie and found her in the tearoom.

"Bradley is a natural with the children, and his intuition is in sync with Micah and Maeve. I've overlooked what's happening in his life and how he came to be here and alone at Christmas. I don't believe he mentioned having siblings back home."

Searching for volunteers, he spotted Clifford Winters at the front door. "Cliff, we're full to the rafters; could you please help Sadie in the tearoom and also ask Lola to come over and lend a hand? Just light chores like taking orders and pouring the tea."

"Of course. Do you mind if I use the desk phone?"

Cliff was about to call but saw Lola Turnbull on the sidewalk with her cart and rushed outside.

"Lola! Lola! It's good to see you. Do you think you'd mind coming in to help Sadie pour the tea? There are so many customers and not enough hands."

As he watched her reaction, he saw years evaporate from her face, and she practically giggled with consent. "Of course," she said, "I love to be needed!"

Winters stashed her cart in the cloakroom and eased her through the congestion to the tea counter.

"You now have another elf, Sadie!"

"And I have two aprons ready. Cliff, could you clear tables as they empty, and Lola, when the trays are ready, send Bradley up to the kitchen for more baking. We need gingerbread, Christmas cakes, and cupcakes with the top decorations."

Lola stayed right at Clifford's side while she re-oriented herself. Within minutes, she was drawn into the store's energy, rushing about in the presence of old friends and customers.

Mr. Grayber took a chair at a corner bistro table then stepped to the counter for a mince tart and a hot spiced cider.

Returning to his table as an interested observer, he began jotting, then sketching on a notebook from his pocket. He tapped his toes to the chatter and looked up, smiling and humming. On page after page, he drew depictions of toys and puppets that caught his fascination and the faces of people that passed by.

Clearing a nearby table, Winters spotted Grayber's notebook, seeing a remarkable pencil portrait of Lola that took his breath away.

"Sir, you are certainly talented. That is a perfect likeness of my friend." He leaned for a closer look. "You have captured her inner beauty as well as her expression and smile. Would you consider selling it to me?"

Clifford wondered if he'd been too forthright.

"Ah, I see . . . it's Cliff Winters, isn't it?"

"Yes, you have a precise memory for names."

"I'm in Stowe for other matters, but on the side, I do freelance sketching and journalism about matters that inspire me. This town inspires me in the spirit of caring that people show for each other."

Clifford's eyes hadn't left the drawing. "I'd like to buy it if I could."

"I don't usually sell my work, but I see this strikes a personal chord with you, so I insist that you take it as my gift. Outside, folks talked about the magic of this place, and I am becoming a believer. The fellow at the door, Mr. Hancock, said that we are all here for a reason, that nothing here happens by accident."

Clifford glanced across the room at Lola. "Yes, she is more special than I realized. Rudy and his family are the heart of this town, and you are right; we have magic here in Chimney Ridge. Thank you kindly."

A clatter of dishes falling behind the counter took Winters away, concerned that Lola could use his help. In the whirlwind moment, Grayber became aware of the snappy tune in the background with elves dancing as they worked. Shoppers were humming along, and an old gent was whistling with his shoulders swaying to the rhythm.

Grayber noticed a young woman in the archway with a baby and looking for a table to rest. He gestured that he was ready to sacrifice his spot and stood to hold out his chair for her.

"Please, Madame, I was about to leave. May I order something for you from the counter?"

"That is very kind of you. If you could please tell Sadie that Chrissy is here with her baby, she'll know what I need."

He wondered how he might recognize the person who was Sadie. "It must be the white-haired, smiling lady dressed as Mrs. Claus."

Meandering through the crowd, Grayber stopped to examine the puppet display, then observed the elves' joy as they threaded through the store. As one kicked up both heels high in the air, he nodded, "I will remember this scene to sketch or even paint."

He moved close to those waiting to place personal cards in the Wish Box and watched others dipping their hands into the Deeds Box for an envelope.

A teenage boy made his selection first, then an older man, who appeared to be of lesser means. Each looked stunned to read the request but then honored to have accepted the responsibility.

Grayber approached the teenager. "Ah, son, it is generous of you to want to take a deed. May I ask what is burdening you that you felt the need to oblige."

Benedict Thompson looked up, and he flushed at first, appearing uneasy.

Grayber regretted his approach as he realized the lad was about the same age as the son he had lost years before. They both had rusty blonde curls and freckles across the nose. He was confused to feel a stab of pain in his heart.

"I'm sorry, son, I didn't mean to intrude. You see, I'm from out of town, and I find this selfless process fascinating. I do freelance journalism and thought it might make a heartfelt article to draw attention to true benevolence."

"I'm not embarrassed, sir. On the contrary, I'm grateful and proud. You see, I am a benefactor myself from a previous year."

"It's fascinating to me," Grayber said. "Can you tell me more?"

"I am now a violinist. I could never have hoped for my dream to come true if it weren't for these boxes. It must have been someone very kind and unselfish to do such a thing for me and open the doors for my future. Perhaps one day I'll be privileged to meet that person and thank them for this gift."

"I heard the story of a boy with a great musical skill that was blessed with a violin on Christmas. Would that be you?"

Benedict blushed as if he'd become a celebrity. "Indeed, I am the recipient of that wish, and now I feel I can return a deed to someone else."

"I'm not asking what request you chose, but I'm curious about the cost of selecting one of the deeds."

Benedict stood taller as he spoke, knowing this was a moment of greatness for him. "It forces you to look deep into yourself to find what you can do for others. It will take thought and effort, but I'm confident that I can do this."

"Well, then, I'd look foolish and selfish standing here if I didn't fall into line and do the same, right?"

Benedict offered his hand in friendship. "It's been an honor, sir." As Grayber's eyes followed him, he knew the exchange had stirred a different type of emotion and a deeper understanding.

Rudy saw Grayber near the boxes, and his curiosity eased him closer. "Merry Christmas, and welcome to our Christmas store, sir!"

"I understand you are Mr. Hancock. I realize you are busy now, but could I impose on you for an interview while I am in town? I'll write an article highlighting the goodwill of Chimney Ridge."

"Call me, Rudy. We are busy day and night, Mr. Grayber, but if you join me for a walk tomorrow, you'll get a clear picture of what is happening in our little town."

Grayber was grateful and nodded his agreement. At that moment, a customer was tugging at Rudy's sleeve for assistance and nudging Grayber out of the way.

"Tomorrow morning, at eight o'clock?" Rudy offered.

As Grayber made his way to the door, he contemplated what was special about these people. They differed from what he knew; everyone was cordial and eager, gracious to others who could become benefactors. Those arriving looked at ones leaving as if they shared an intimate connection, each coming to participate.

"It would be improper not to make an appearance at Hancock's Emporium at Christmas," Grayber whispered. "And unforgivable not to engage in the Wishes or Deeds."

13

Seeking a Benefactor

It was a half-hour past closing when Rudy and Sadie finally locked up for the day, overwhelmed at the response from the families, children, old folks, young mothers, and anyone that ventured into the crowd of shoppers to participate.

Glancing around the store, it was apparent the shelves needed restocking with merchandise and adjustments to decorations.

Bradley straightened the puppet stage that Micah had arranged beside the counter. "As a kid, I'd have loved one of those," he mumbled. "Marionettes, too, with their imaginary world. I was brought up on the fascination of TV muppets."

"What's that, my busy elf?"

"Nothing, Rudy, I was just talking to myself."

Bradley was piling chairs and washing the tearoom floor when Rudy came to dismiss him.

"Bradley, let the night elves finish up. It's time for a bite of supper," Sadie smirked as if a magical group of helpers would appear from thin air and make it all go away.

"Night elves?" Bradley said.

Rudy winked. "You'll see. By the time you come down in the morning, it will be ready for another day. A new troop of elves will arrive before we open. Haven't you wondered how Sadie and I could do all this?"

Gathering empty baking trays, Bradley followed Sadie upstairs, and at the kitchen sink, he poured a warm bath of suds and rolled up his sleeves.

"It will only take a few minutes for my warmed-up casserole, Bradley," she said, but he grasped the pot out of her hands.

"I'll do that. We all have big appetites tonight but put your feet up, Sadie. The dishes can soak while I warm up the pot."

Her shoulders sagged with fatigue, and falling into the armchair, she let Bradley put the footstool under her feet.

"I see you were raised to be considerate. You must have parents and grandparents at home that would miss you greatly."

Bradley didn't answer but continued at the stove. A few minutes later, he realized Sadie hadn't said another word but had dozed off.

He turned at Rudy's heavy footsteps on the stairs, and they both looked at Sadie, asleep with her spectacles still on her nose. Rudy covered her with an afghan from the sofa, then leaned and kissed her forehead.

"Sit down, Bradley; it's just you and me unless Sadie wakes up. She loves all the bustle but forgets we're getting older. We appreciate having you here." Rudy dug into the chicken casserole and took a buttered bread slice from the stack.

Bradley chuckled, "I'm beginning to think I could be an elf. It's given me the chance to see people for who they are despite their hurts and pains. Understanding the theory of Wishes and Deeds and watching them happen in real life has opened my eyes. We are all alike, needing the same simple things in life."

"That's good, Bradley. If you're not exhausted, you could give me a hand as I'll take today's wish and deed requests to the workshop and deal with them."

Rudy gently rubbed Sadie's hand to awaken her. "Dearest, let me help you to your bed. We've taken care of everything for tonight, and you need some rest." She didn't resist and disappeared down the hall with Rudy's arms around her to guide her steps.

When Bradley unlocked the boxes in the Emporium, he found more requests than he could have imagined. He carefully placed the contents in the canvas pouches under the counter.

In the dimness of the empty store, he breathed in Christmas smells of cinnamon and pine and sensed the veil of history and mystery that surrounded him. In the open quietness of the store, he looked around and felt its grandeur, then joined Rudy in the workshop.

A great book lay open on the workbench in the basement, and Rudy was already writing the day's entries. From behind, his white curls eased over his collar, and his red cardigan hulked over his broad shoulders.

As Bradley gazed at this remarkable man, a shiver of gratefulness ran up his spine.

"Bradley, did you see the fellow that came in by himself

and sat in the tearoom? He was an outsider but exceedingly inquisitive about Chimney Ridge. He claimed to be a journalist interested in writing an article about our town, but I'm not convinced as he was sketching and drawing in his notebook."

"Perhaps an artist?"

"He'll come for a walk-along tomorrow to see the first-hand workings of our town at Christmas. He wants to write about the magic of our Emporium. Frankly, I believe he is a questioning soul searching for his own heart."

"I saw the man. He blended in with other customers and didn't particularly draw my attention. I can't say that I had an opportunity to talk with him as we were so busy with customers."

"Yes, indeed we were. I rely on my instincts a great deal in understanding people."

Rudy looked over his glasses, smiling at his earlier assessment of the homeless lad.

"The fellow's curiosity was from deep inside, perhaps wounded years ago with coal in his stocking."

"Coal in his stocking!" Brady said. "I haven't heard that expression since I was a little boy. The mere mention strikes a cold spot and emptiness I wouldn't wish on anyone."

"It's unfortunate that folks sometimes dwell on the past, forgetting to take full advantage of today or make tomorrow more satisfying for themselves or others. The fellow I'm talking about was Mr. Grayber; my gut tells me he is in a position to make a difference to our town this year. I'm rather good following my instincts."

Rudy absent-mindedly continued making notations in the book as he routinely opened each envelope.

"Ah-ha! Here's a letter to Santa pleading for a puppy.

That shouldn't be too difficult for us, Bradley. And I think I know who's house this will be going to; it is one of those situations that has come full circle. It's signed Emmeline Newman."

Rudy handed the childish writing to his elf to peruse.

"Shall I put that one in a pair of mittens for the church tree?" said Bradley.

"I think that would be suitable. And there's another one here that I had put aside. Lola Turnbull asked for a bicycle for her newsboy, Henry Parker; he needs it to do his route. I was going to ask Mr. Hoskins at the hardware store, but it could go with the mittens as well."

"I'll put the puppy request in the blue mittens with the snowman on front and the bicycle in the green mittens with the reindeer."

Rudy added to his notes then dropped the mittens into Sadie's basket for the Reverend.

"Now, this one is more difficult. Here's a wish for an invitation to join a family for Christmas dinner." Rudy rubbed his temples. "Of course, we always welcome folks without a home or family to join our table at Christmas dinner, but then it would be too obvious that we had intercepted the wish which would interfere with the Santa magic."

"Perhaps we should put it in the Deed Box, and someone will take it and make it a reality. Two birds with one stone, right?"

"That's a better idea," said Rudy. "Unfortunately, we are getting many more wishes than deeds selected."

"It can go to someone in the church congregation. It doesn't cost anything to invite someone to join family dinner."

"When someone requests a family dinner, it is not because they are hungry for food, but they are yearning for family. Special memories with others are what last. I predict that a benefactor will step up before Christmas."

As Rudy spoke, an idea was dawning on him. "Remember I said everything happens for a reason? I believe Philip Grayber has a deeper purpose for being in Chimney Ridge than simple curiosity. I've lived here for years and know pretty well everyone, and I can't think of a soul without a place to sit on Christmas Day. So I'm guessing it must be a newcomer."

The final task was the flood of letters addressed to Santa at the North Pole, with each one deserving attention and a thoughtful reply.

"What are the guidelines to reply to these, Rudy?"

"We do our best at reassurance, but as everything isn't always possible, we make the best equivalent. Keep a list of names, requests, and the resolution."

"With so many, how will we reply to all of them?"

"Tomorrow, Maeve and Micah will help with the replies. You can put unusual toy requests in the mittens; however, the standard will go to Mr. Hoskins at the hardware store. We have an open account there, and if it isn't covered otherwise, he will bill us. He always notifies the parents, and we've never had a slip-up."

"Do you mind if I write the reply to Billy McKenzie? He wants a toy garage with an elevator from Montgomery Ward that he'll share with his brother, Donnie. Billy even included a tear-out from the catalog, so he gets the right one!"

"Ha! That saves us time. Tomorrow, take that by Hoskins and ask him to place the order. If I were a kid, I'd have that on my list too. Growing up, I wished for things like a spinning top, toy soldiers, a Red Flyer sled, and a baseball glove."

Rudy was reminiscent in thought, and his mind took him back in time. "Every kid loves going through the Christmas catalogs."

14

Charity Begins in Chimney Ridge

Before breakfast, Philip Grayber departed the Stowe hotel room and wheeled his Rover on the snowy road to Chimney Ridge. He was outside the Emporium a few minutes before eight, feeling oddly excited about his day with Rudy Hancock.

Grayber had expected to meet a friend in Stowe for a romantic ski weekend at the Von Trapp Lodge. On the day of his arrival, the lobby was filling up with families arriving to enjoy the Christmas ambiance. He waited beside the tall tree near reception for his companion but didn't receive any call of regrets.

Concerned, he phoned her residence in New York, and she candidly said she wouldn't be coming and had made other plans. The rejection wasn't unexpected but was still devastating.

To make the best of his weekend, Philip sought the advice

of a housekeeping matron who insisted that he see the fantasy in Chimney Ridge. That led him to bring his burning curiosity to yesterday's queue.

Through the night, Grayber couldn't dismiss the town's care for others and desired to belong. "If only I could bring strength and cheer to others who may feel abandoned as I felt when a little boy."

He had dreaded the onset of the festive season for many years, of people caroling, tinselled trees, feasting in gatherings, and even children frolicking in the snow. Instead, he threw himself into make-work activities, finding excuses not to participate and becoming reclusive from social events.

Something had happened in the few hours as he waited outside the Emporium; observing the happy chaos inside the store, he felt part of something, something big that stirred his inner self.

He saw a belief in the faces of the locals that what revolved around this store and town was enchanting and inspirational.

A strange feeling overcame him, like the first day of school or the excitement of meeting new friends and hearing about their summers and plans. Oddly, he had felt more at home at boarding school than in his family's house with unattached servants.

"What was that the little girl said about Mandy Carson, that her secret wish had come true—I want to know that. Can I find Benedict Thompson and hear more about his violin? I want to see those green elves singing," Grayber blabbered on to himself. "I want to have a Christmas heart!"

Philip was disappointed that the main street shops hadn't yet opened; however, he found a bank's ATM kiosk and withdrew a large sum of money. Taking a stack of envelopes from the tray, he stuffed his day's assets into his breast pocket.

Rudy arrived in the store at precisely eight to turn on the lights and restock for the day's business. He had forgotten the time until he saw Philip Grayber waving from outside, waiting to begin his partnership for the day.

"Good morning to you, Mr. Grayber. We have a pleasant snowfall again today, and you look eager but cold."

Rudy took a closer look at his new comrade but didn't see the man behind the façade. The eyes looking back concealed a lonely man wanting to discover his mission in life.

"It's a momentous day to be sure, Mr. Hancock, but since we'll be a duo, please call me Phil. I intended to come bearing hot chocolate, but it seems Chimney Ridge is a sleepy town, and I couldn't find a coffee shop open."

"Come in and warm up; we'll have it perking soon. We are always eager for an extra pair of hands."

As Bradley and Sadie came down minutes later, they hushed at the sound of rustling in the storeroom. From the darkness, Micah called out, "Good morning, folks," looking like he'd slept there. He pulled on his elf hat with a jovial grin.

"You must excuse me," he said as he scampered away to restore the rest of the shop before opening. "I need to finish some important elf work."

Rudy's assumption was correct that Grayber would follow at his heels like a shadow. As he went about tending to his preparations, he chattered incessantly about the things he was doing and barely glanced at his counterpart.

"Phil, you see, we tended to the boxes last night, and my assistant Bradley will follow up with Mr. Hoskins at the hardware store. For Mrs. Carson, we need to know what she can supply for the church mittens for Sunday service."

Grayber listened to every word and nodded each time as if in agreement.

"Calendar, my calendar," rambled Rudy. "Saturday is the retirement center's Christmas party; oh yes, I must meet with Middleton regarding the Fezziwig affair."

"Fezziwig," said Grayber, then repeated it louder, enjoying the musical sound of the word. "Fezziwig!" he barked.

"Ha-ha. You're getting into the spirit," Rudy said, "Just look at our packed calendar. The soup kitchen's charity auction needs attention, and someone must delay the pet adoption. And I can't forget that Sadie needs help for the bake sale." Rudy let out a sigh, and Grayber nodded his understanding.

As Bradley returned the boxes to the front, he passed the men with packages in both arms. He acknowledged Grayber with a shake of his head. "Good morning, Mr. Grayber; it's nice to see you here again."

"Ah, you're Bradley, the new elf. I noticed you yesterday, and I'm impressed by how well you interact with the little ones. I've never given the career of being an elf much thought, but I'm finding it quite enticing and educational," Grayber said.

Just then, the doorbell jangled as Lola and Cliff merged into the store to help. Lola was embarrassed that she leaned on a cane for support but resigned to her new arthritic gait as Cliff instinctively reached out to support her.

"Good morning, my good friends," said Rudy, "meet Mr. Grayber. He'll join me today to learn how we go about Christmas. He is impressed about the town's festive spirit and learning about the magic we manage to achieve."

Graber extended a handshake. "Yes, I believe I met Cliff outside the store yesterday. And this charming lady must be Lola. I was grateful to be a party to the conversation outside; it gave me a beautiful insight into the town."

"Our pleasure to know you," Cliff said. "Help yourself to coffee, Mr. Grayber!" He poured a cup for Lola, knowing to add her cream and sugar.

The newcomer surveyed the scene with enhanced admiration for Rudy and Sadie and enjoyment of the elves. Marveling at the intricate décor, he felt like he was ten years old beside his grandfather.

As his long-forgotten memories surged, he wanted to become involved in the magic of Chimney Ridge.

"If I could have my childhood back, I would have enjoyed Christmas more and paid attention to those around me."

Grayber fidgeted in his pockets for an envelope filled with currency from the bank machine and dropped it discreetly into the Deeds Box. With his eyelids closed, he sighed with a sense of satisfaction he hadn't known in a long time.

Rudy paused for a quick gulp then spun on his heels. "Grab a take-out lid and bring your's with you, Phil; we've got to get a move on." Peering over the others, he called, "Sadie, anything I should ask Mrs. Middleton? We're on our way over there now."

"If she asks what food I'll send for the Fezziwig, tell her cabbage rolls. Otherwise, she can call me."

She continued placing pastries on the bakery shelves under Grayber's eyes. He wanted to linger and watch the café come alive, but the reality was at hand.

"Phil, grab a take-out lid and bring your coffee. We've got to get a move on," said Rudy. "But you need one of those fresh from the oven, so grab one while you can. Sadie never sends anyone out of here on an empty stomach."

Rudy led the way in his oversized parka, marching quickly toward the town hall built after the Revolution. At a corner, he came to a sudden halt and turned left.

He spewed more historical recitations at each building, starting with the newspaper office that still ran its 1950's presses. Then they had a moment to consider the Musket & Thistle's British Tudor influence, spiced up with Rudy's tales of the minutemen who stayed there two-hundred years before.

Rudy allowed a one-minute lecture of the French Victorian architecture of the antique store and told humorous recaps of the inns and taverns, each claiming notable American figures who had bedded there.

The Fidgets and Whims toy store turned on its outside speakers as they passed it, piping jolly tunes out onto the street.

Grayber was already walking too fast, trying to keep up with so much trivia to take notes, but Rudy's words continued to accelerate as their pace picked up.

"We need to run over the Fezziwig program for timing and speakers, volunteers, equipment, and anything else that comes up. Middleton is organizing it, and if you are around the Saturday before Christmas, you can join the committee. That's not an invitation we give out too lightly, so embrace it."

Phil took a swallow of hot coffee in stride and sputtered, "I hadn't thought that far ahead. But, of course, I'll be happy to help while I'm in town."

Rudy's finger waved as he spoke. "Always think ahead if you want to get something done. Sadie and I prepare all year for December. I make toys in the workshop, she organizes events and recruits volunteers, and we search crafters in the community for unique homemade items; those sell best and hold lasting memories. Everything comes together, and there's always a surprising member of the community that comes forward to make it all happen."

Rudy's brisk gait was intended, and Grayber did his best to keep abreast. He was used to being the leader, but today he was the follower and found it to his liking.

Meanwhile, Cliff broached Lola about the Metcalfe's dinner invitation later in the week. He was tentative, wondering if she would notice the sudden pairing.

She could see that he was nervous and noticed that he had combed his silvery hair precisely. It didn't scare her to see him differently, but it was surprisingly reassuring.

"My goodness, Clifford Winters. Is this a date?" Her eyes searched, hoping for his acknowledgment.

"Well, not exactly. Surely you don't think of me in that light, would you? Could you?" He paused and waited, afraid that he had made the suggestion too soon.

Lola didn't laugh, and she didn't decline. Instead, she gave him a gentle smile and patted his hand. She did her best to downplay the suggestion while harboring a long-forgotten sensation of being needed.

"You've always been one of my favorite people, Cliff.

Surely two old folks can go about town visiting their friends without everyone talking about us."

Sadie overheard the pair in the coffee shop and showed a smug grin. She would boast to Rudy of her matchmaking instincts later that night when she could finally have his attention again.

15

The Walk-about

M rs. Middleton darted about the community center basement, checking lists and schedules as she juggled phone calls and issued tickets for the upcoming ball.

As Rudy entered, she was wearing her feathered button hat with her particular pearl hatpin again. It was rare that he'd ever seen her without it, except at the Fezziwig, where she let her hair down and turned into a wildcat, in his opinion.

"Thank goodness, it's you, Rudy!" Mrs. Middleton exclaimed, seeing the pair at the bottom of the stairs amidst the chaos. In front of her were banquet tables strewn with piles of organized papers and supplies.

"Slow down, Myrtle; everything will be sorted out. First, I'll introduce you to Philip Grayber. He proposes to write an article about the Christmas miracles that come to our little town. You are my first stop this morning."

Myrtle straightened her dress and patted her hair with the expectation that her picture might be taken. She adjusted her plastic poinsettia corsage, then sighed in resignation that Grayber didn't sport a camera around his neck.

"It's a pleasure to meet you, Mrs. Middleton," Grayber said diplomacy. "The ball is a tremendous undertaking, and surely you deserve a great deal of credit for your efforts." To complete the ploy, he withdrew a black notebook from his coat.

"Middleton?" he said. "Mrs.—?" Instead of making notes of her achievements, he adeptly let his pen mimic her personality into a sketch.

Mrs. Middleton continued the spiel of her years of experience and community efforts to impress the society reporter, speaking quickly with a high pitch of authority in her voice. Rudy waited for her to break so he could urge her to expedite the ticket process.

"Myrtle, we've got a lot to cover. Do you have ticket batches for me to drop off around town? We're off to see Mr. Hoskin, and he has offered to sell tickets."

"They're right here, Rudy, but please look over the program as I need it for the printers. Our mayor will be Fezziwig himself, as he is every year. He'll give a welcome speech with pertinent announcements, and the Reverend will say grace before dinner. As the emcee, Calvin Klegg will take band requests and give a speech about the history of the Fezziwig."

"Are enough door prizes lined up?"

"Oh, yes, and all donated by merchants and a few artists. Just this morning, Kennedy Farms offered a Christmas Eve sleigh ride on his farm for auction. Calvin will pick winners after the meal, then thank the groups that dedicated themselves to the success. They're the usual ones every year."

Mrs. Middleton rifled through the table's papers, oblivious to the phone ringing in the background. Finally, she spun around to someone in the back. "Lillian, will you get that?"

"You can advertise the band now," Hancock said. "They call themselves Finding Fathers. They're working men who entertain on weekends while searching for lost children. We'll place posters in stores in the downtown area."

Grayber was stunned to hear the band's motivation in traveling around New England. He wished there was hope one day for him to locate his own son; however, he was poignantly aware that his boy had perished on the ski slopes during an avalanche.

"Having the confidence of finding a lost child makes each day worth living," Grayber thought to himself. "I suppose there is some truth in that for me every day, and the pain lessens a wee bit."

Rudy absent-mindedly handed a bundle of posters and tickets to Grayber, who was silently assigned on the spot to be a valet this morning.

"So, this is what it's like to be the right-hand man," Grayber thought to himself and laughed.

"Myrtle, do we have a list of last year's music requests to give to our new group?" Rudy asked. "Draw one up and include the traditional dance songs we all know."

"Last year was a regular band, and we let them come up with their own. But I'll get a list of our lively ones ready."

"The bandleader assured me they would be obliged to our needs. Jazz and swing are their specialties and the main criteria I gave them. Oh, and perhaps a bit of fiddle. They already knew about the Sir Roger de Coverley Scottish jig, the Thread the Needle, and the other ones—those are paramount."

"Oh, dear! Will they handle it all?"

"Don't fret, Myrtle. They're highly recommended. Once you've finished with the program, send it to the printer on Disher, and I'll have them picked up when they're ready."

Rudy turned to Grayber in a new thought. "You'll need a proper outfit, Phil! We dress according to the Fezziwig period, thoroughly Victorian."

"I hadn't considered that yet, but of course. I have no idea where to get an ensemble or even acquire a date."

Rudy roared his pleasure. "You need to have a wee chat with my wife; she'll take care of all of that. Sadie and the tearoom ladies are very resourceful. I've never heard of anyone arriving without an ensemble or someone to accompany them.

"I don't mean to scare you, Phil, but this town operates as a whole, and they don't consider gossip to be harmful, just helpful."

Hoskins was standing outside the front of his hardware store when the duo arrived. "Good morning, Rudy. Your elf, Bradley, called ahead, so we've been expecting you."

Hoskins looked curiously at Grayber. "You must be today's shadow? I don't believe that I've met you before."

Phil stretched out his hand. "It's my pleasure to meet you, Mr. Hoskins. I'm Philip Grayber; I'm at the Von Trapp Lodge for a holiday. My family has been in New England for centuries, but I'm afraid I had overlooked the necessity of visiting your charming town."

"Ah, at the quaint lodge in the mountains. Then you must

be learning to yodle!" Hoskin said. "It's much easier than herding sheep."

"Of course, what's the point of staying at an alpine chalet without acquiring a new skill. Next, I'll have to consider one of those alphorns that make the bull call," Grayber said, humored at the silliness of his comment.

Rudy said, "My goodness, will wonders never cease? I've been wanting a lesson; perhaps later, you could give us some pointers."

The sounds of motorized toys and trains encircling the window displays triggered more memories for Grayber. Right away, the creaking of the hardwood floor was comforting, and the smell was nostalgic with a combination of old cardboard boxes, furniture polish, a hint of diesel, and a touch of opened paint.

Hoskins' notebook was open on his counter, and he stared at the raft of papers and rolled posters that Grayber held.

"I have a list of names waiting for tickets. What have you brought for us, Rudy?"

"I have a packet of tickets, and this envelope has some North Pole requests that need your help, Walter. Let me know your out-of-pocket expenses, and we'll even up later."

Grayber had stepped back to let them conduct their business, but he struggled not to show his deception on hearing this discussion, and he eased forward between the men.

"Mr. Hoskins, Mr. Hancock. Would you please let me take care of any expenses? It's the least I can do to thank the townsfolk for exposing me to this experience."

Rudy was taken aback. "That's extraordinary, Phil. Surely you don't fully comprehend the extent of our efforts at

Christmas. Many in the community lend helping hands and donate whatever can be spared. It wouldn't seem fair to impose our financial burdens on a visiting journalist."

"I can't say I fully grasped the extent of magic here at first, but I assure you that it isn't any imposition. I ended up in your town by a sequence of events that I hadn't anticipated—."

Grayber paused to explain himself. "Then I heard your young elf explain to a patron that each one that benefits from this spirit of giving is not here by accident. I am also now convinced that I have been brought here for a purpose, something I don't fully understand yet."

Rudy was struck by hearing the words that he'd told Bradley when he brought him in from the cold.

"Ah, you were wise to listen then, Phil. I do believe that is the truth, and fate is bringing us together one way or another."

"Then call it fate or destiny if you like, but I have my reasons for wanting to take care of the expenses for Mr. Hoskins," Grayber stated, his gentle determination warning Rudy not to challenge his decision.

From his jacket, he pulled out another envelope filled with money and a business card. He laid them on the counter in front of the two men.

"Does this convince you of my sincerity?"

Rudy picked up the card, embossed with a familiar name, Grayber Enterprises, New York.

"Ah, so you are not a journalist, Mr. Grayber. Under the circumstances, perhaps you could explain this game plan to us," Hoskins said as he opened the envelope. "Good gracious, this is an extraordinary pile of money!"

"I insist that my explanation must remain in confidence."

Grayber looked over his shoulder for privacy. "As you know my company's name, you will be aware that we distribute toys, games, electronics and many things that would be appropriate at Christmas. I inherited the company from my father, and growing up, I had every tangible item I could ever want or need. Still, I didn't have a loving family or community as I see here in Chimney Ridge.

"I didn't share a childhood with siblings, aunts, uncles, or family friends. Instead, my Christmases were in luxurious hotels with staff to provide decorations and dinner. The gifts from my parents came in the form of checks. I would have been happier with personally chosen mittens.

"In turn, when I had a son of my own, I tried to make it different and fulfilling. But ten years ago this Christmas, I took him on a ski holiday that ended in tragedy. Let's just say that I understand the name 'Finding Fathers' more than you can imagine."

Rudy was unprepared for the empathy he felt. "I'm sorry for your pain and anguish. I'm beginning to understand, Phil. You will be an enterprising journalist while you are in Chimney Ridge, and we assure you it will not leave our lips. Remind me back at my workshop that I have a letter to share with you."

Hoskins was tongue-tied as he stared at the business card. "I'm at a loss for words, but you are welcome in Chimney Ridge, especially at Christmas every year. I believe I met your father at a merchandise trade show in New York years ago."

"He passed away some time ago, not realizing what a joyful season this can be. I appreciate your confidence."

Soon after Rudy and Grayber set off on their walk-about, Bradley departed the Emporium with an errands list and last-minute instructions from Micah and Sadie.

The first stop was at the Carson house to pick up a box of mittens. He still wore his elf cap from the store, and when Mandy Carson opened the door, her eyes widened in surprise.

"You're an elf! Isn't it too early for a visit?" Mandy teased, offering a broad smile minus her two front teeth.

"Why, you are Mandy Carson. Your letter has been dispatched to the North Pole; I saw it go myself."

"I know that it did, and my Christmas wish has already come true." She dropped her voice to a whisper. "I asked for Mr. Jackson's son to be sent home from the war."

"What a remarkable request! You are very thoughtful," Bradley said as he absorbed it. "But surely there is something that you wanted from Santa for yourself."

"At Macy's, I asked for a Barbie cut-out book, but when I thought about Mr. Jackson, I changed my mind. Then, one day at the Emporium, Mr. Hancock explained to someone that Christmas is not always under the tree, but the best presents come from the heart."

"Mandy, you're wise for your age."

"I will soon forget about the Barbie stuff, but I'll never forget about Mr. Jackson getting his son home for Christmas. It's a gift that lasts."

Bradley looked in amazement. "Certainly, your request to Santa was a secret, but you say it has something to do with Mr. Jackson's son!"

"Oh, yes, I guess I can tell you since you are an elf and all." She angled closer to whisper in his ear. "I couldn't believe it myself, but I saw with my own eyes. The army jeep came a few days ago with Mr. Jackson's son. Santa gave me my wish!"

"You are a marvelous little girl, giving up your own Christmas request for the sake of your neighbor. Isn't it rewarding to do something to improve life for someone else?"

Mandy beamed with satisfaction. "Indeed, it is. This will be my best Christmas ever for the rest of my life."

"I appreciate that you shared that with me. I will always remember what you have done."

Mrs. Carson was near enough to overhear them, and Bradley looked up, ashamed that he had prodded into Mandy's secret; but Mrs. Carson smiled tenderly.

"You must be here to pick up the mittens, Bradley. I have some bundles by the front door. Let Mr. Hancock know that some ladies will help me give you more in a few days. I understand you'll need a batch for Sunday for the church."

Bradley went on to see the Reverend with a box full of mittens. He was familiar with the church from nights when the overflow of mission beds was set up in the basement.

"Good morning, Rev. Atkins; Mr. Hancock sent me with these mittens."

"Ah, yes, you must be Bradley Rimble, the new elf. Come with me, and I'll show you where we are setting up the Christmas tree."

16

Confessions of the Heart

When Rudy returned, the Emporium was packed with customers, and he listened to the contented hum amongst the staff. Micah and Maeve were leading a training session for newly recruited students about unpacking merchandise and pricing tags in the back.

Sadie waved for him from the coffee shop, and he dodged to her through the crowd.

"We got a call this morning, Rudy, and Gary is on the afternoon train from Chicago. I told him someone would be at the station to meet him. Unfortunately, a delivery truck is waiting to unload at the back door, and it's going to be tight for time."

"Ah, it will be good to have him home for Christmas, and we could surely use the extra pair of hands."

Cliff and Lola were still loitering in the coffee shop, serving at a slow pace. "If you'd like, Rudy, I can go to the station for Gary," Clifford said. "As the store is open late, it might be hard for either of you to get away."

Chimney Ridge was the sort of town where everyone helped out their neighbor, and Winters had been close to the Hancock family as the children grew up. Gary was the oldest of the two children and most like Rudy, eager and hands-on.

"I'm grateful, Cliff," Sadie said. "Gary will be glad to see you."

As she jotted Cliff's pickup details, Philip Grayber arrived for the end of his shadow day. "Rudy, you said you have a letter to show me?"

"I always keep my word, Grayber. Sit down first for a healthy bite, and then I'll take you to my workshop."

"We still have some hot beef barley soup," Lola said, "and I'll warm up the popular cheese tea biscuits."

"They'll warm me up too," said Grayber. "Rudy enticed me to attend the Fezziwig Ball, but I haven't brought anything appropriate to wear, Sadie. Where could I arrange something suitable?"

"We'll put together a dazzling ensemble so you fit in as you should. But be prepared for britches, a brocade vest, a long coat, and knee stockings with button shoes and buckles!"

"How unusual," he said, "but so much fun too."

"Yes, and most importantly, you will celebrate and dance more you can imagine."

In earshot, Bradley was intrigued about the costumes. He knew from the first night that the Fezziwig was a highlight, but it hadn't occurred that he would be included until this moment.

"Bradley," she called, "will you and Mr. Grayber come upstairs with me?"

She winked at Rudy. "I'm taking the boys up for a fitting. Can you spare me, love?"

She continued to the hall's end on the second floor and reached up to pull a lever in the ceiling.

"There's another level above us?" Bradley said. "Are there more mysteries I haven't seen?"

"Watch your head and stand aside as the ladder comes down."

Sadie flicked a wall switch, and the upper floor flooded with light. Climbing the pull-down stairs, they followed her to the third-floor attic lined with racks of costumes, dressed mannequins, hat boxes, theater shoes, trunks, and three full-length posing mirrors in the outer circle.

"A menagerie!" Bradley declared.

In the center of the room stood the likeness of Mrs. Fezziwig on a wired hooped frame in a pyramid of crinolines, bustles, petticoat underlinings, well-worn ornate heeled gold slippers, and a carefully arranged golden bouffant.

"Good gracious, this is fabulous and improbable!" Grayber gasped. "I've never imagined an attic could hold so much mystery. This is the type of hidden room that children dream of visiting, and here we are!"

Sadie stood back with her arms crossed, making visual measurements. "How tall are the two of you?"

"I'm five foot eight," Grayber offered.

"The last I measured was a half-inch shy of six feet," Bradley confessed.

Sadie lifted the player arm of a Victrola on an antique table, and carousel music filled the room. Then, the animated mannequins began to move.

Grayber slowly turned in a circle taking in the room's exhibition.

"My wish, Sadie, is that I could have had the privilege to be part of Chimney Ridge years ago when my son was alive to have given him this thrill of a lifetime."

Sadie was struck by the tragedy. "I'm sorry, Phil. I can see how very much you miss him."

"He'd have liked this, and I'm equally inspired. Young and old alike benefit from imagination."

"Come over here, Phil; I have something in mind for you."

They stopped at a rack of silk tapestry vests and tailcoats. "Ah, the dark green one! Yes, it will be perfect for you." Bradley waited as Grayber strutted, adjusting the coat around his girth.

"Gary will be home tonight, Bradley. He'll bunk in with you, and I think you two will get along splendidly. He'll only be home for a few days and will spend most of it in the workshop at the carpentry bench."

Sadie thumbed through the hangers. "Now for yourself, let's see. A midnight blue waistcoat."

"Come now to the shelf of rugs to complete your Dickens look. There are toupées, bald caps with curls out the side and back, or full wigs in ponytails. Have a gander. However, if you're opposed to wearing those, you can make modifications with Brylcreem and a part down the middle. My son's hair is longer, so he prefers a ponytail with a ribbon, and it looks just awesome."

Engrossed in the activity, Bradley barely heard Sadie depart. "I'll leave you two here for a bit. I need to go downstairs, but I'll be back."

"I'm sorry to hear that you lost your son," he said, realizing Mr. Grayber was still there. It strikes me how selfish I have been about many things."

"Why is that? I suspect there's no reason to feel that way."

"Mr. Hancock is aware of my circumstances. I left my home immaturely two years ago as my pride had been offended."

"Many of us act impulsively at times, not just when we're young."

"I have learned while being here at the Emporium that little things are unimportant," said Bradley, "and I regret my actions."

Grayber offered more humble advice from the mirror as he pulled on some khaki pantaloons.

"Bradley, you remind me very much of my son. I was grateful for every day I had him in my life. If he could see this, he'd be blown away by the magic that surrounds us here. You are right; we can hold too many regrets in life and not embrace the joys of today."

"The time I've had here with Rudy is the best in my whole life," Bradley said. "He is more than Santa Claus; he's a teacher, a friend, a mentor, and much more that I can't put into words. On the night he found me huddled in a bus shelter, he brought me in and said I would be an elf with a purpose to complete.

"I felt I had been rescued, and that greatness was before me. I am torn now, wanting to continue to be part of this special time but regretting that I haven't relieved the pain of my parents. I know they love me, and I owe them an apology."

"You know, you and I are somewhat in the same pickle," Graber said. "That's why we are standing here together. I dread being at home alone at Christmas. So I enticed a lady to the mountains for a ski holiday to avoid the family feasts and frivolity.

"I didn't mean to come to Chimney Ridge; I was sort of sent here. And you, dear boy, I thank you for reminding me of family and regrets, and I hope you will consider me a friend in the future. This time we spend will never be forgotten."

Bradley's voice cracked with emotion. "Family and friendship are the greatest gifts, but I took that for granted."

Sadie reappeared to assess their selections. "What a fine pair you two are. I agree with your choices; now the only parts left are the dancing shoes and a damsel for each of you."

"But, Sadie, I fully expected to be working at the ball and not participating," Bradley objected.

"Nonsense, there's no such thing."

"Mr. Grayber, you will be fulfilling a wish for a lovely young mother in Chimney Ridge. I am letting the cat out of the bag but believe it to be necessary. We have a shy widow who hasn't been to the Fezziwig since her husband died five years ago. She's one of the nicest and prettiest women in town. You may have heard of her son, Benedict Thompson, or Dick as we call him. He was desperate for a violin and lessons, and that wish was fulfilled.

"She wishes to attend the ball but is too shy to make herself available, but we have decided that you will be her escort this year. You will make a handsome pair, I assure you."

Grayber couldn't object when Sadie had said that it was decided. He'd learned already that there was no use in arguing with a Hancock.

"And for you, Bradley, my daughter Gabriella will be home a few days before the ball. She doesn't like going with her brother as her date. She is quite beautiful and takes after me," Sadie said with a grin and a nudge. "It's the duty of a senior elf!"

"Then it would be my honor."

17

An Old Friend Reunion

B y the time Bradley and Philip Grayber came down the steps into the store, Rudy, Maeve, and Micah had restocked the toy shelves, and the remaining clerks were about to leave. As the doors swung open, Cliff and Gary entered.

Gary was tall, with curly hair like his father, a square jaw, and the sparkling eyes of his mother. His face glowed with the same eagerness.

Sadie rushed to him. "Gary! My goodness, you've grown." Dropping his duffle to the floor, he swept her up in his arms, and Rudy waited for his turn.

"Thanks for picking him up, Cliff; it was kind of you."

"We had a chance to catch up on the last school year. It's only at Christmases that we get time to talk."

Clifford shuffled from one foot to the other, twisting his hat in his hands as he focused into the tearoom for a hopeful sign that Lola was still there.

"She's gone home for the day, Cliff. She's got to take care of that sweet boy, Otis. You know, her beautiful retriever."

"Otis, yes," he repeated slowly.

"It's a shame she'll need to part with him; he's an old dog, but he still needs a house and a yard and someone that likes to snuggle. We kept him here once for a few days when Lola went to her sister's funeral, and he was a charmer. Lola said she'd meet you here in the morning."

"Well then, I'd best get on my way," Cliff said. He reluctantly nodded at the door, and Gary stepped forward with his hand.

"Thanks for picking me up, Mr. Winters. Promise me our annual game of checkers while I'm here?"

"Yes, but I won't go easy on you this time."

Walking the few blocks to his house, Clifford stopped to look down Spruce Drive, where he would turn to go to Lola's. The lamppost illuminated his steps, and he found that he was looking down the street to the next corner.

At that instant, he realized he longed for her companionship and to see her reassuring face.

He had another block to go to get to Settler's Row and his empty house. He took in the moonlight and looked differently at the chorus of chimney stacks smoking in their evening hearths while he reflected on the joy of the family's reunion in the Emporium.

Nearly every house, mainly two-story or federal-style with shutters, was trimmed along their eaves with strings of colorful lights. Even the picket fences and sculpted hedges were intertwined with festive lighting.

Looking in at the gingerbread houses with families

around their Christmas trees, he had a wave of envy of belonging to a family and home.

He dreaded the end of every day, making the walk to the street behind the old hardware shop. He knew the sounds of the door creaking as he opened it nightly into the quiet house that seemed too often to have a permanent chill in the air.

Trudging onward, he was heartened that he would see Lola in the morning, and it gave him a boost of inspiration. Straightening his back and lengthening his stride, he turned toward his house with a sudden warmth in his heart.

Stepping into his parlor, he was struck by the obscurity of his home. He hadn't lit the living room hearth in more than a year, and the double glass doors straight ahead hadn't been opened since Thelma's passing. As she could no longer climb the stairs, he had made modifications to the library and converted it to a bedroom.

Cliff meandered into his kitchen for a cup of tea, and it suddenly occurred to him that he wasn't looking for the ghost of Thelma, but instead, he longed to see Lola tomorrow.

"Perhaps a soothing tea will help me relax. Sometimes it takes a moment to look at your environment through someone else's eyes and see it the way it is. It's time I make some improvements."

Plodding upstairs to the hallway to the bedrooms over the Emporium, Bradley felt like an intruder, sleeping in someone else's bed. Gary was intuitive to Bradley's reaction and was quick with an agreement.

"I see you've been sleeping on the bottom bunk. I outrank you and should boot you out, but I won't do that. At my school dorm, I've become accustomed to the top anyway," Gary teased, and his smile broadened. "I'll enjoy the company for a few days. I'm afraid I talk quite a bit, and it will be good to have a listener."

Bradley was immediately at ease. "Well, then it's good that I prefer to listen than talk! I'll never tire of hearing old stories about Chimney Ridge."

The roommates chatted into the night about schools, friends, festivities, the decades of Christmas tradition, and the townsfolk, then returned to talk of Rudy and his magical boxes.

"It's like living at the North Pole. You'll be here on Christmas Day, won't you, Brad?"

"That's a huge decision, and I'm working on it, Gary. I wake up in the mornings feeling like I've been cast in a movie, and this isn't all real. But, when the lights go down, it will be the same world that I left two years ago."

"It *is* like a movie," Gary said, "but can be so much more with its impact on others and ourselves."

"I need to take responsibility and make amends to many people. If I stayed here, I'd be avoiding folks that are the most important in my life. Being here has been an escape. At night, when I remember my parent's faces, it's clear as a bell, and I know they love me and will forgive me. In the morning, it is hard again."

"You know, Bradley, you are one of many elves who have come here for Christmas, and you won't be the last. That's part of the ongoing mystique; it will never cease. I've been fortunate to be raised in this fairytale, that we can improve everything with doses of kindness.

"I went to school to get away and disprove that theory, but it is true. One day I will assume the inspiration of my parents and provide this same hope to another generation.

If I am honest with myself, I look forward to it, and I do love being in the workshop and being creative with my own imagination."

Bradley lay on his bed with his hands cupped behind his neck looking into space, as thoughts of his family and his future weighed heavily on him.

"Listen, Bradley. Listen, isn't that beautiful?"

The house had fallen silent, and the only sounds that Bradley could pinpoint were the light wind blowing against the window, the shuffle of slippers in the hall, the waning aroma of Sadie's baking, and then something else, quiet and sweet.

"What is that?"

"That's the sound of a home, of belonging; it's my parents holding hands and the whispers of the sandman waiting to settle wishes and dreams upon us. Please take a deep breath, then slowly blow it out, letting your limbs release to the ends of your fingers and toes. Let yourself fall into dreamland."

Hearing gentle snoring, Gary whispered, "Goodnight, Bradley Rimble."

It was early, and the sunrise had not yet risen over the horizon when Cliff Winters set his feet on the cold floorboards beside his bed.

However, this morning he did not wander to the window to check if other lights were on across town to absorb his misery. Today, he had a purpose, and his heart was pounding.

Lathering up his shaving cream, he stood before the bathroom mirror whistling to the tune of 'Buffalo Gals.' Pale blue-grey eyes looked back at him, but today, he noticed a sparkle emerging.

Satisfied that he'd done a thorough job on the three-day-old whisker crop, he slapped on a stinging aftershave with the favorite scent Thelma that had given to him a long time ago.

Tonight was the evening a group of volunteers would take their gifts and bakery treats to the retirement center, with a haphazard orchestra of an accordion, ukelele, and flute. Others would use bells and tambourines to keep in rhythm.

It occurred to Cliff that last year Lola had volunteered and brought Otis along. The pooch was a favorite with residents, starting up more visits. He was likened to a therapy dog in the enjoyment he brought.

"Ah, Otis, he belongs with Lola. She's been brave, not grieving over the loss she'll endure leaving her apartment. I know how attached one becomes in the simplest of everyday life."

In his living room, he realized that he had no Christmas decorations this year or an inviting atmosphere, and he remembered a trunk in the drawing-room where the baubles and festive trinkets were stored. Abandoning his usual caution, he dug in, looking for newer decorations he could appreciate this year. First was the musical lantern that played 'Here Comes Santa Claus.'

"Good gracious, I forgot, I'm supposed to wear Rudy's red suit at the retirement place. Perhaps he's changed his mind. The old folks don't need Santa; it's the fable that enamors us. But I guess I can heave out a few more festive Ho, Ho, Hos."

The kettle whistled on the stove and jerked him back to the reality of his morning chores. He popped a slice of bread into the toaster and glanced at the clock. "Only six! I wonder when Lola starts her day?"

He recalled Grayber's sketch in his coat pocket and carefully laid it on the table. He patiently looked at each feature, then rooted through a closet for an empty picture frame. Satisfied it was suitable, he centered it on the hall bureau.

With the dishes washed and his counter polished, he stood in the front foyer with his coat, hat, and gloves, watching the clock tick toward seven. He listened for the town clock to strike to make it official that the town was awake.

Opening the door, he greeted Henry Parker, who was arriving with his newspaper bag.

"Good morning, Mr. Winters!"

"Mornin' Henry, are you the only one on the street up right now?"

"Ah, shucks no, sir. I've got to make my deliveries before I catch the school bus."

Walking toward the row of apartment buildings on Spruce Drive a few blocks off Main, Cliff stopped at the corner phone booth. He dug into his pockets for the change he had scooped up from the hall bureau and was nervous while it rang.

"Hello, Lola, are you up? I'm an early riser and was wondering if I could take Otis for his morning walk. You were at the tearoom most of the day yesterday, and I thought he deserved some attention."

"Good morning, Cliff; I'm definitely up. Come by for a cup of tea, and we can walk Otis together."

He smiled to himself, his gait quickened, and he found he

was whistling that tune he'd hummed in his morning shower. When Cliff arrived at the apartment building, he rang up from the entry hall for the security lock to release, then climbed the stairs in double steps forgetting he was not so young anymore.

"That was quick!" Lola's voice chimed as she waited at the open door. Otis was wagging his tail and trying to squeeze between her legs at the sight of company.

"I was anxious to get out for a walk this morning," Winters mumbled. "As I get older, it's harder to get a good night's sleep, not that there's any noise."

"I know what you mean; the nights can be long living alone, with many things on my mind these days."

Her face flushed as she settled on his blue eyes. "Come in and rest yourself; the tea is almost ready."

"Tea! I smell muffins."

"We get our fill of treats at Sadie's, but I like the aroma of baking in the house, and I won't be able to do that much longer."

The delicate touch of a woman's decorating lifted Cliff's spirits instantly. A small, tinselled tree with a string of lights was on a tea trolley in the hall, and a poinsettia was blooming at the table's center.

"It looks like Christmas here, as I'm afraid I haven't bothered much," he confessed. "Lola, I was wondering if you'd mind if I could be your date to the Fezziwig this year. I know we'll be busy, but I'd like the reassurance that I came with someone. With you, I mean."

Her soft laugh was like music. "That will be just fine, Cliff. I'll have to borrow from Sadie's closet as I haven't anything elegant left in mine."

Otis begged Cliff for ear rubs and attention as Lola set the teapot to steep on the table.

"I made lemon cranberry muffins to go with our tea. I only make these at Christmas, and you'll have to come back another time if you'd like blueberry."

Her voice drifted away, realizing that there wouldn't be another time.

18

Matchmaking for the Fezziwig

Consumed with the unfinished Deeds, Rudy and Sadie talked about the day's developments late into the evening.

"You've had remarkable progress in matching people for Christmas, Sadie. It's always best to defer to your instinct in those delicate matters."

"It seems to me, dear, that Philip Grayber and Lydia Thompson are destined to meet and find the companionship they are missing. He suffers the loss of his son, and Benedict is an inspiring young man. Although the wish for a family Christmas dinner was anonymous, I'm convinced the handwriting is the same. So, our trickery would contribute to fulfilling a Deed!"

Rudy enjoyed Sadie's rationalization as she prattled on. "The situation with Cliff and Lola is well in hand. Their friendship strengthens every day, and I planted the value of a canine companion in the household. I expect he'd like that. Time is short, but the heart waits for no one."

"You've become quite the sleuth, Sadie. I have nothing to lose by relying on your woman's intuition. What do you need me to do?"

"Arrange to get Lydia and Grayber together one way or another. There is already a kinship with Benedict, so you could work something there."

Rudy concocted excuses to call Lydia Thompson but was nervous about presenting his plan. Finally, he dialed the Thompson home.

"Lydia, could I impose on you to assist us at the retirement lodge Christmas outing Saturday evening. I saw Benedict and realized that we hadn't seen you for a while. We invited him to play a violin solo, and perhaps you'd like to hear him perform."

Lydia was flattered by the invitation and assured Rudy that she would be on hand to help. "I am familiar with the lodge. I was a trauma nurse at the hospital in Stowe, and after that, the lodge would call me to help out in emergencies."

"I remember that you were a nurse. I have a friend visiting from Stowe who is also helping out. I suggested that he pick up Benedict with his violin beforehand, and you are welcome to have a ride. He's a lonely fellow and would appreciate the company. I'm trying to encourage him to come to the Fezziwig this year."

"Who is your friend?"

"His name is Philip Grayber, a splendid fellow, and he's already met Dick."

"That would be fine, Rudy. I'll look forward to the occasion."

The call flustered Lydia, with a mix of excitement and lack

of preparedness to accept a ride from a stranger. After she hung up, Rudy's words resonated. "Ah, he's setting me up for a Fezziwig date!"

For several minutes, she sagged into an armchair. The conversation nagged at her, then struck reality. "Philip Grayber, no, it couldn't be!"

Rudy gave a thumbs up to Sadie to acknowledge his success. "Now to square this with Grayber!" He took a deep breath at the predicament he created for himself from his meddling.

As the muffled sounds of lathes and polishers filtered from the workshop up to the main floor, Rudy was comforted that Gary had returned to his place at the carpenter's bench, joined now by Bradley.

He eased down the stairs quietly, not to disrupt them. With their heads together, the boys were studying the lathe as it spun and spat out bits of wood and sawdust. Bradley was intrigued by the process that wasn't elementary to him.

"Good morning, fellas. What's the project this morning? Is it befitting of elves?"

"Yes, Dad. It's one of yours. I showed Bradley how to turn the wood, then looked at your charts at a few pending projects. I didn't think you'd mind if I gave out some pointers."

"I'll never turn down optimism or willing hands."

With his magnifying spectacles, Rudy examined the workmanship. "Oh, you are assembling pieces for the nutcrackers. Excellent, as the store's stock is thin. Nutcrackers of all sizes are selling fast as they are symbols of good luck and buyers like their unique personalities. Inspirational sayings are all ready upstairs to attach to each one."

A wooden drummer boy was drying on the shelf before a final coat of varnish, and Gary saw his father studying its detail.

"You know, Dad, he's always one of my favorites, but this one is special for Mom., so I made it for Christmas."

"You take after your grandfather, and he would be proud. I'll leave you to the woodwork, Gary; however, I need to recruit Bradley's help for the morning. The gift baskets for the retirement lodge are ready to fill, and Micah and Maeve are backlogged with Santa's mail replies. Mrs. Atkins from the church will help, but we need to get more hands."

"Redirecting mail for Santa? It's like I'm in a dream," Bradley said. His eyes darted with a vision of the jolly elf sliding down the chimney, and he imagined tiny faces as their fantasies would be realized.

"As a boy, I begged to sleep under the Christmas tree to see Santa. My pleas went unanswered, but I tried to stay awake, listening for hooves on the roof or fussing in the chimney. All those hours I spent waiting and believing, and I am here now in this miraculous process."

Cliff and Lola had taken over the coffee shop even before Sadie's request.

Lola was in a white lace blouse and an embroidered vest with ruby buttons. She put on a freshly laundered Christmas apron and sighed her contentment at being so much at home in the store. Once again, she remembered the feeling of being needed.

Giggling, she whispered to Sadie, "Cliff and I are going to the Fezziwig together, so I'll need to see your garret for a costume. It's been years since I was at a dance, and I'm not sure I remember how to corkscrew or thread the needle. I'm certain that my arthritis won't co-operate, but I'll still enjoy this so much."

"I've saved a perfect ensemble just for you, with ocean blue princess lines and ivory petticoats. It's not too heavy, and it will make your eyes dazzle, dear."

"Why, Sadie, you're a rascal! I do believe you have partially concocted this."

Lola toyed with her friend, enjoying the tête-a-tête. "I'm almost overwhelmed at the attention. Cliff came by this morning for coffee, and we walked Otis together. We're invited to the Metcalfe's for dinner, and he's picking me up for the lodge party."

"Every day is a new adventure, Lola, so we must try our best to keep up."

Rudy opened the morning doors a few minutes early as Philip Grayber was waiting outside. Rudy and Sadie locked glances knowing it was incumbent to confess about Lydia Thompson.

Grayber was ready to put himself to work right away with his newfound friends, and he took the liberty of shuffling things over on the counter for a box he carried under his arm.

"Leaving New York, I put this in my car trunk without any deliberate reason. One of our distributors offered it to me, but I didn't have too much Christmas in my heart at the time to realize how helpful it would be. Go ahead, Rudy, open it."

Tearing off the tape, Rudy found four dozen identical small boxes, with miniature houses encased in snowing atriums. A family of figurines and an illuminated Christmas tree were inside every home.

When Rudy pressed a button underneath, snow fell with the music of 'We Wish You a Merry Christmas.'

"There should be enough for each member at the lodge to get one with their package. It'll add some spirit to those who need a boost this season."

"Oh, that is fantastic!" said Lola, hearing the music. "In my books, that beats socks, soap, or a cookie."

"That was kind of you, Phil, and those folks will be appreciative. Chimney Ridge is fortunate that you arrived here for Christmas.

As they chatted, the doorbell jangled. Rudy froze, seeing the new arrivals, but Sadie caught the awkwardness. "Hello, Lydia! How nice to see you." Grayber didn't see the glances and made his way into the coffee shop.

"Hello, Sadie," Lydia stammered. "I spoke to Rudy on the phone, and he brought up the Fezziwig. I got to thinking that it's been ages since I went to any of the seasonal affairs in town. Benedict and I have been on our own for a long time, and I never thought of social life." Grasping for words, Lydia now wished she hadn't come.

"Please sit down. We'll have a cup of tea and catch up," Sadie said, nudging Lydia's elbow toward a table.

Philip Grayber was ordering his breakfast at the pastry counter when Lydia stopped in her tracks. She studied his side profile, trying to unravel the puzzle.

"Excuse me," she said, "I think we've met before. I'd remember your voice; at least my instincts would tell me that."

Grayber turned around and paled. "My goodness! I'd never forget your face. I'm afraid your name has slipped from me, but you were my Florence Nightingale."

Sadie pulled a chair from a nearby table for Grayber. "You should sit down; you look like you've seen a ghost."

"I'm sorry to bring up painful memories, Mr. Grayber, but I'll never forget you and your son. There was so much love in the hospital room that night, and we did our best. Again, I'm so sorry."

Nearby eyes and ears were now turning to the spectacle.

"I've never thanked you for your kindness to my boy and me as well."

Lydia nodded. "The night was terrible when the avalanche struck."

"I recall every second like it was yesterday. He was behind me one second, then gone. I dug with my bare hands, and the rescue unit was there quickly to pull him out." Philip Grayber's words faded as he thought, and Sadie set a glass of water for him.

"They performed CPR and said he was alive. A tremendous rush of relief, and I didn't hear anything they said after that." He stopped again.

"With understanding eyes, Lydia said, "You might be confused about what's going on, Sadie. I was a trauma nurse at the Stowe Hospital the night they brought in Justin Grayber. I was with the doctor and Mr. Grayber at the boy's bedside when he passed away."

Philip Grayber reached out to Lydia Thompson for a comforting embrace. "Thank you for helping us that night. I should have properly given my gratitude, but it was easier to pretend that night never happened."

Sadie was trembling to see this beautiful reunion, and Rudy reached for her hand. "I see that we don't need introductions."

She leaned against his chest, and he wrapped his arms

around her. "I can't imagine losing a child!"

When the emotion was exhausted, Lydia and Philip parted, with an understanding they would go to the lodge together and be partners at the Fezziwig.

Rudy knew he needed a distraction. "Philip! I have yet to show you my workshop. Will you spare a few minutes?" Before descending the stairs, Grayber took one more look at the door hoping for Lydia's return.

Gary was at the workbench painting a marionette, below a rack with a large Pinocchio and an Orphan Annie. Grayber paced along the wall's shelves, examining the rows of nutcracker dolls in varying finishes.

"I don't believe it," he said. "Their eyes follow my movement as I walk."

"They come to life in our minds," said Gary. "Mr. Grayber, would you like to see the toyshop?"

"What imaginations you and Rudy have! Could you show me how Pinocchio performs? As a kid, I watched Andy Pandy back in the '50s. He lived in a picnic basket with his friends, but I was captivated that the wires controlled every move."

"Andy Pandy? I don't think I've heard of that one," Gary said as he gathered Pinocchio with its wires to demonstrate its agility.

"You see, Gary, my background is from a toy company, and I thrill in how an inanimate object can become expressive with some mechanical persuasion. An umbrella can open a skirt, or a suction cup will secure a base; a spring can do any number of deceptions."

Rudy was intrigued by Grayber's interest. "Philip, we don't have an Andy Pandy, but if you would like to take

Pinocchio, he would be happy to have a home with you."

"He's a fabulous puppet for some child at Christmas, and unfortunately, I couldn't take that from you. Perhaps another time when you're not so busy, we can talk about a special order. But if you don't object, I have my Polaroid, and I'd be happy to take pictures."

"Well then, Phil, come and see the control area where we process Deeds and Wishes and how we make sure all these dreams come true."

"There's no place I'd rather be," Grayber said, then caught himself as he thought of Lydia.

19

Chimney Ridge Comes Together

The whirlwind of events was accelerating more each day, and the Emporium's traffic queued down the block for gifts and last opportunities for a wish or deed.

In the lines outside, children stretched on tiptoes for a glimpse of an elf inside. Word spread that a contingent arrived in the night, that the workshop was busy and the sleigh sacks were getting filled.

Gary enlisted his old school chums to stock the store shelves on the final Saturday before Fezziwig, and Cliff agreed to wear the red suit in a chair set to receive the children near the mailbox.

Grayber had delivered a box of Christmas coloring books, crayons, and paint-by-number sets, and every child that whispered in Cliff's ear was rewarded with their choice and a peppermint stick.

With the Fezziwig only a few days away, Bradley faced

the reality of finding his way home for Christmas, needing to make amends to his family. Gary, his confidante, saw the changes in his new friend and sought out his father with the dilemma.

"Dad, Bradley is carrying a significant burden and is in a quandary. Do you have an intention for him? I shouldn't ask, but has he made a wish or taken a deed?"

"Bradley has allowed himself to be fully involved in the Christmas spirit and giving back to Chimney Ridge. He assured us of his help through the season, and I know he is good for his word."

"And when he's finished?"

"He's a fine young man and is beginning to see his way clear to return home. It will be at his own time, but as you know, our mission is to resolve wishes however we can. I have taken some discreet steps to ensure that will happen for Bradley."

Gary's eyes brightened that a plan was afoot.

"If Mother were listening, she would say that patience is a virtue and that I should have faith in how the wishes and deeds come full circle. I've struck a kinship with Bradley and would like to see him find his way."

Rudy knew that the answer would arrive in time for the Fezziwig Ball.

"Patience, Gary, you'll see that everything falls into place."

Everyone said the lively Saturday night retirement lodge Christmas party was the most successful they could remember, with a dozen volunteers distributing gifts and leading carols that seemed never to stop.

In the corner, Lydia and Grayber were stoking up a

trusting friendship and finding something more profound as they bonded in the shared, intimate moment in Philip Grayber's life.

Oddly, it gratified Grayber that he had bonded even more to Chimney Ridge tonight through this unexpected encounter.

Benedict Thompson played a heart-rendering version of 'O Holy Night' and 'Once in Royal David's City' to Lydia's proud delight.

Otis refrained from naps and circulated with his gentle canine manner, satisfied with constant head rubs and oohs and aahs for being such a good boy.

Later Cliff and Lola requested a site tour, and the house manager showed them the guestroom assigned for Lola's arrival at New Years. Its color was drab, needing decoration, and she would share the room with a newcomer from Coventry.

She couldn't look at Cliff, fearing that he would notice her reaction. He gently took her hand. "It will be alright, Lola, trust me."

She did her best to put on a brave face. "You've been a good friend, Cliff, and I've appreciated the attention in helping me get to this point. I'll need to make my journey from here on my own."

He stopped and faced her, admiring her bravery and seeing her hidden pain. "Lola, may I ask if you put a request into the Wish Box at Hancock's?"

She was alarmed that the Emporium must have deceived her. "How would you know about that? The purpose of those boxes is to help our neighbors, correct? Henry Parker has helped me all year. His family is having a hard time, and he needed a bicycle for his paper route."

Cliff regretted he had forced her secret. "That was a thoughtful request you made on Henry's behalf. I didn't know you had made a wish; I just wondered."

He paused, then added, "I participated myself, Lola."

"It would be rude of me to ask what you made as a wish," she said.

"Every year, I secretly took a Deed card from the box. This year I found one that struck a chord of coincidence with me."

"I'm glad for you, Cliff," she said. "We don't know when our blessings will come."

"Lola, I've started to pay attention to details about you. It began with your situation that you were searching for a home for Otis. Rudy gave me an envelope and said he didn't know what it was, but his instinct said it was for me. Of course, I had to trust in Santa Claus!"

"Yes, I have asked for a family for Otis."

Lola sighed, relieved that the truth of her stress about loneliness had not been fully exposed.

"It breaks my heart to part with him, as he's my only family in Chimney Ridge. I couldn't bear the sound of opening my door and not seeing his wagging tail and feeling his sweet, warm face nuzzle into my hand. We take the simplest things in life for granted."

"I understand what you are saying. An empty house is not a home unless you have people in it that smile when you enter. These last weeks I've looked forward to the times we are together. My house is empty; however, my heart has become full."

"I should have paid more attention to your progress this past year," Lola said. "I'm sorry if I didn't offer the support you needed."

Cliff was still holding her hand, and his voice was stern but gentle. "This event will continue without us," he said, "but we need to talk; please come back to my place instead."

"You are an extraordinary friend, Cliff."

She felt the weight of the world fall from her shoulders but was quiet on the drive to the Winters' house. When he helped her out of the car, she hesitated.

"I'm sorry, is this uncomfortable to bring you here?"

"Oh, no, Cliff; it's just that I haven't been inside your house since Thelma's funeral. I can feel that she still lives here."

A momentary expression of pain crossed his face then vanished as he looked upon this precious woman that already meant a great deal to him. She looked fragile yet beautiful and watching her filled his heart.

"Let me make some tea, and you'll see that there is no one here but me."

While Cliff fussed in the kitchen, Lola settled on the sofa and surveyed the room.

"It needs a woman's touch," she mused. Then she looked at the bureau across the room and couldn't believe her eyes. Cliff had a framed sketch of Lola, herself.

"My goodness, Cliff! Where did you get this?"

He rushed to the living room at her voice, forgetting he had centered Grayber's sketch of Lola so he'd see it every morning.

"I hope you don't mind, Lola. That fellow that follows Rudy around town sketches folks as he chats. I saw him drawing this in the tearoom and bought it on the spot. It is beautiful to me!"

"You are a gem, dear Cliff. That is the sweetest thing I've

seen in ages."

As the party continued at the lodge, Benedict Thompson was still receiving accolades for his violin performance, with Lydia standing, reminding many that Dick was her son. Impressed with the talents and nature of the young boy, Grayber but couldn't stop noticing comparisons with his son.

"Benedict, you were indeed blessed to receive your violin, and you responded by dedicating yourself to master it in your training. Amazingly, this came about from a Christmas wish and someone acting on it. I've seen the tangible results of the magic your town embraces, and I'm glad I'm here to be part of it."

"My Mom told me about your son, Mr. Grayber, and I'm so sorry. I would like to have met him. I understand he would be about my age."

"Yes, and you'd have been friends, I'm sure of it."

"Anytime you'd like to talk about Justin, I'd be happy to learn about him. He'd be proud to know how you are helping our town. From now on every time, I look up into those mountains, I'll remember him."

"No one has said that to me before, and you can't imagine what a release you have given me. Most folks avoid mentioning someone who has passed on, fearing they will invoke painful memories."

"I understand that, sir."

"It's not the *hard* memories I want to hang on to, but it's the happy ones. It is rare that anyone even mentions my son's name. You are a remarkable young man."

Lydia watched these two men with awe, not wanting this warm moment to pass.

"Perhaps, Philip, you might like to come back to our

place and join us to decorate our Christmas tree. We usually leave it until just before the Fezziwig. We'd be happy for the help."

In the morning, the Emporium was in a frenzy. It was the day after the retirement lodge party and the Eve of the Fezziwig.

Rudy was glad that Gabriella had arrived home late the night before. She had begun her junior term at college in Hartford and forgoing visits home due to part-time work to pay her tuition.

Gabriella was barely twenty, with golden curls like her mother and teasing in her eyes. If there was any mischief to be had, she was in the midst of it.

"Hey, Pops, I can see that you're busy, but I'm overdue for a dance!" She propped herself directly in front of her father with her arm up, pretending to be wearing a full dancing gown and waiting to be twirled. "I could use some practice for the ball."

"Here in the store?" In a pickle, Rudy glanced at Sadie to rescue him. peer

"Have you met Bradley?" Sadie asked and scanned through the crowd for his green hat."

"Oh, the cute elf over there by the post box? Where did you find him?"

"Don't be cheeky with him, Gabby; he will be escorting you to the Fezziwig. He is a fine young man, and you should be lucky to earn his attention."

"He's not so bad at all," she said.

Bradley has helped us these past weeks, and we need him at the Fezziwig. You could also teach him a few dance steps."

"What's his story?"

"Your dad rescued him during a storm. He's been obliging and fully into the festive season and has supported everything on the schedule. But his personal tale is for him to tell, not me."

Gabriella sized him up again from across the room. "Yes, Mom, I'll see that he has a good time."

20

Fezziwig Arrives

In the tradition of every Eve of Fezziwig, the church bells rang out across the town as if the Second World War was over. Patrons were lining up in the downtown shops for last-minute costumes for the ball, and up and down the main street, horns honked, and spirited passengers waved from open car windows.

In anticipation of the next day's extravaganza, the keenest residents already donned their apparel to march in a spontaneous parade, practicing two-steps and swinging arm-in-arm.

The late afternoon roads were clear for a convoy of 1920s convertibles cruising the main route despite the winter chill. Notable figures in their finery waved from rumble seats, holding banners to advertise the ball.

Some progressive merchants seized the opportunity to tout their products over a blow horn. The hoarse voice of radioman Carl Bench bellowed, "Last chance to get your Christmas corsage at Wiggins Five & Dime. Two-for-one while they last. A brand-new shipment of men's slip-on galoshes just arrived. Get your size today before they sell out."

Down the block, Carl started again. "Dawe's Groceteria has a ham special that you can't miss out on or their bakery's iced Chelsea loaf. A reminder that this is the last day to order a fresh turkey for Christmas. And, of course, Monday is Ladies' Night at the Musket & Thistle Tavern."

Warmed by his coffee thermos, Carl continued, "Ladies and gentlemen, Mrs. Middleton reminds you that parking at the community hall is limited. School buses will be running a free shuttle from Hancock's Emporium, the Baptist Church, and Geddy's Gas Station every hour, beginning at six. If anyone cannot obtain shuttle service, they should call any pick-up points to make other arrangements."

The sounds on the street overpowered the Christmas music piped inside the Emporium as folks with reservations for outfits from Sadie's attic lined up at the cashier's desk.

Sadie shook her head to Rudy. "Gabby must roll up her sleeves and pitch in too. She's off galivanting with her pals. I'm counting on her to help me with the ensembles in the attic."

"Lola is doing a stellar job hosting the garret and distributing the costumes. If Gabby comes back to help, all the better. It's good to have her home. She's been away from town since Easter, and we must remember she has her own life."

"I suppose it is under control," Sadie said.

"Did she meet Bradley yet?"

"She knows who he is, but only from a glimpse across the floor. He will take it in stride."

"The evening promises to be eventful for him," said Rudy.

"He'll be surprised when he becomes aware of your deception."

"Ha-ha, yes, and it is for his own good. I don't feel guilty setting up Bradley and the unsuspecting band members. I don't think it will be a distraction, but if it becomes one, it will be meaningful."

"Rudy, it's all in the spirit of Christmas."

In a flash, Sadie disappeared to the attic to assemble her costume. At the dressing table, she laid out her makeup and examined her hairdo in the mirror.

"If I had a Christmas wish, I would want the last twenty years back. I would be kinder and more charitable." She pinched some color into her cheeks. "I'd have taken better care of my skin, and my friends."

An image appeared of a beautiful young woman standing beside her. With disbelief, she looked again, seeing Gabriella in the doorway in a yellow princess dress with pink ribbons and white gloves to her elbows.

"My goodness, Gabriella, I didn't hear you come in. For a moment, I could see myself in you, and it gave me a pleasant pause."

"Oh, Mother, you are beautiful in your gown tonight. I couldn't miss the Fezziwig, and I'm glad I'm home in time. Nothing compares to this night's happiness when the community joins together. Charity doesn't matter about age, agility, or fortune."

"You are a vision, Gabby. If you take a ringlet wig, I'll

give you a hand with the hair ribbons."

Gabriella embraced her mother. "I love you, Mom. I've been counting the days to get home and see you."

Minutes later, the pair returned from the attic in full costumes from Charles Dickens' characterizations. Rudy, Bradley, and Gary were becoming equally decked out in Victorian garb in the shop below.

Rudy's vest was buttoned tighter this year from gaining a few pounds since last Christmas. The horse-hair Welsh wig was itching his scalp, but he ignored it and straightened himself to look like an authentic Fezziwig.

"Come on, Fezziwig ladies, we'll be late for the ball," he said. "You don't expect your pumpkin to wait for you indefinitely."

Sadie's face was flushed from taking the stairs faster than her costume should allow. "Gary, would you fetch the casseroles from the refrigerator. I'm due at the church to serve the band's dinner, and Myrtle will be anxious."

As Rudy retrieved Sadie's cape from the cloakroom, he tugged at his buttons to find some leverage. "Gary, if you drive your mother to the church, I'll go with Bradley and Gabriella to the community hall to be on hand when the organizers arrive."

Although confident with his plan, Rudy had butterflies, knowing that the bandleader's introduction was ahead. The bandmaster had assured him everything was in order, but the importance of the music was secondary to his scheme. He couldn't wait to see the moment of recognition.

Bradley was stunned at Gabby's beauty as she appeared from the stairs in an array of ribbons and curls. They locked eyes unexpectedly, and he reached for her cloak to drape her shoulders.

"We are about to have a fabulous evening, Bradley. And I believe you're blushing."

"Indeed, I am. You are lovely, Gabriella."

She tucked her arm into the crook of his, and he moved as close as he could without standing on her gown.

As the moonlight drifted through a spattering of clouds, a dusting of light snow created an appropriate Dickens backdrop as two town criers boasted of the arrival of Fezziwig.

Behind them, on the main street, horse-drawn carriages carried participants in eighteen-hundred apparel. As the parade wound through the town, it grew with more costumed partiers at every corner.

"Hear Ye, Hear Ye," a crier called. "You are at this moment ordered to attend the joyful feast and exuberant party of the Fezziwig about to commence. Our Lord Mayor so orders it. Onward ye citizens of Chimney Ridge; ye must proceed to the community hall!"

The festival had been officially kicked off, and the town hall's clock echoed six times.

Rudy found that the band had accessed the hall at the community center but had already left in their bus for Mrs. Middleton's dinner at the church. He was adjusting the microphone when Mayor Leadner approached him wearing a balding wig with rows of curls around the circumference.

"Good evening, Ewan." Rudy said with thumbs up. "You're as dapper as ever and a supreme Fezziwig, if I do say!"

Captivated as the evening's celebrity, Leadner spun a full circle so Rudy could compliment him on his attire with knee stockings and buckled dancing shoes. Mrs. Leadner tugged at her skirts in a proper curtsey but restrained with the bulky weight of her wigs and feathered bonnet.

"Rudy, we are primed and ready for this evening. Of course, there will be an introductory procession when the evening officially opens, I presume?"

Leadner pompously puffed his chest. "We will enter with fiddle music and clapping, and as I take the hand of my lady, we will kick up our heels!"

"I have an updated program for you. I'll introduce the entrance first; then, after your jig, you'll open the evening with your speech. Mr. Klegg will conduct the program from there."

Leadner reached into his vest pocket for a raft of papers. "Yes, yes, I have it here."

A troupe of musicians was assembling near the stage in bow ties, vests, and top hats, and the bandleader sported an instrument case under his arm. Rudy glanced across the room for Bradley's whereabouts, then introduced himself.

"We are grateful you could accommodate us in your schedule. As I explained, our usual group abandoned us unexpectedly, as they performed here for many years. I hope you were treated to a proper feast by the church ladies."

"They fed us well indeed; it's gratifying to get a home-cooked meal on the road. We haven't been to these parts before, and it allows us to do some leg work. I understand there is a soup kitchen, and the church has a meal and shelter program where we might make inquiries."

"The town takes it seriously to provide for wanderers to ensure they are fed and safe. A young fellow here can tell you more about those services, and you'll meet him shortly. After the mayor's speech, we invite you to explain your mission as you travel around New England. I'm interested in your successes in reunions from your endeavors."

Rudy peered through the newest arrivals. "I don't see Calvin Klegg here yet, but he will be emcee, and Mayor Leadner will lead the party as Fezziwig."

"It's kind of you, Mr. Hancock. From time to time, we receive tips about sightings of children that are distant or missing. A reunion for any family is a celebration."

"Call me, Rudy, please. Are you Keith Rimble?"

Looking into the eyes of an aged Bradley, Rudy saw pain and wanted to explain his underlying plan. He glanced across the room at Bradley, who was in conversation with Gabriella.

"I have a confession, Keith. I run the Emporium, and we encourage folks with heartfelt wishes to make anonymous requests. Others then do their best to fulfill them as deeds."

"A confession, you say?"

"You are not here by accident. I said the same words several weeks back to a lad I rescued from a storm."

Keith frowned. "I see something is on your mind, Rudy. Please get out with it!"

The musicians were tuning their instruments on the stage, and Rudy wouldn't be heard in the noise. He signaled to Sadie to collect Bradley by the arm and lead him over.

The moment's suspense brought joy and anguish as Bradley stared at his father, then looked at Rudy, understanding what was taking place.

"Keith, this is the fellow that can tell you about our soup kitchen and church beds," said Rudy, but his words were no longer necessary.

"Father, I'm so sorry," Bradley said in recovery as Keith, still stunned, clasped him with trembling arms.

"I've missed you so much, son, and I've searched these

last two years wherever we go. I can't believe you are here with me."

In the poorest timing, Mayor Leadner arrived at that moment to introduce himself, putting the reunion on pause.

"Please introduce me to your bandleader since I will be Fezziwig!" Leadner gloated as his chest puffed in celebrity." Rimble was obliging, but his eyes barely left his son.

"We're about ready for the band, aren't we, Rudy?" the mayor boomed.

Bradley leaned to his father. "You'll be tied up with the music, but I'll be here, I promise, as there is much to discuss. I have Mr. Hancock to thank for this."

21

The Party

The liveliest Irish jig opened the evening, with the most excellent measure of oomph, hooting, and hollering to welcome the procession entering the hall.

Over the chatter, Rimble raised his trumpet on center stage and tooted a call to assemble. Then, one by one, the musicians rose to the crowd's applause, each with a few solo bars that built to the entire ensemble.

Responding to clapping hands, Fezziwig tipped his hat, arm-in-arm with the gregarious Mrs. Fezziwig.

Their three twirling daughters were next, then George Wilkins, Mrs. Dilber, and Joe, the housemaids, the cooks, the chimney sweepers, the match girls, the pickpockets, counting clerks, and a long queue of employees.

Lagging in the lineup was the fabled young apprentice, Ebenezer Scrooge, with his fiancé, Belle, then the Crachit family entered, basking in the generosity of Fezziwig's hospitality.

Leadner and his wife leaped through an opening, kicked up their heels in a quickstep, and bounced forward to the center. As petticoats and shoe-buckled locals surrounded them, the scene built into a fever of excitement with whistling and cheering.

The fiddlers then stepped forward with their swinging jive dance tunes, and the crowd surged to the center with the mayor.

First on the dance floor were Phil Grayber escorting Lydia Thompson, and Nate Newman and his wife. Close behind were Micah, Maeve Grissom, the Metcalfes, Hoskins, Partridges, Dawes, Middletons, Parkers, the mailman, and soon every other person that had happened through the Emporium in recent weeks.

Clifford Winters and Lola Turnbull found an alcove table to observe the revelry. "At a slow dance later, we can give it a try," she said, amused at their compromised situation.

A mismatched foursome was at the nearby table, Mrs. Carson with William Jackson and old Mr. Jackson with young Mandy on his arm.

In a sudden move, Leadner swooped up the microphone and bounded to the stage. Already beads of sweat had formed over his brow, and he dabbed it with his handkerchief, then gasped for air to start.

"Yo ho, ladies and gents, let's have no more work tonight as it is Dicken's Fezziwig Christmas Eve! Shutter the warehouse before a man can say, Jack Robinson! Hilli-ho! Clear away, lads, and let's have lots of room for twirling and prancing on our heels as we partake of the merriment."

The mayor's manner was boisterous, monopolizing the

stage. "Set the fiddlers here before me," his high-pitched energy barked. "We'll celebrate our friendship and Christmas spirit." The crowd cheered its approval as the fiddlers struck up another.

"We are bonded together," Fezziwig said. "As one devoted family, we care for each other and our neighbors. 'Tis the season to love one another. Let's demonstrate the lessons our town has learned to share peace and goodwill. So be merry, and let everyone dance!"

As Leadner arched his back and extended his hand, Mrs. Fezziwig, flaunting her excellent corset bustier, pulled up her flouncy skirts with both hands and bounded to him with her feet swinging in the air, surrounded by the three young girls, twirling on their toes.

When the applause subsided, Leadner stretched his arms high, gesturing to come closer.

"Bring on the followers and the clerks, the milkman, the housemaid, the banker, the baker, the brother's friend. Come one, come all, both shy and proud, and we will embrace frivolity and dance into the night!"

The melee joined hands twenty at a time, and with twirling arms, they circled round and round and back the other way, then down the middle and up again. Crisscrossing through the arch at the top each time, partners exchanged until each couple was together again.

"Bandsmen, start up the Sir Roger de Coverley dance. Come everyone, be joyous and merry. Both hands on your partner, bow and curtesy, corkscrew, thread the needle, and run back to your place! All of Chimney Ridge, sing and laugh and celebrate the spirit of Christmas! Feast, and drink to your pleasure."

Bradley was astounded at the sight. "It's an old English

country dance," Gabby explained, "It's from the eighteen hundreds for the Dickens characters in Scrooge.

She gripped his hand and dragged him onto the dance floor, laughing madly. "It's the best way to learn, Bradley; just follow the person before ye. Don't stiffen up, but let yourself go, and you'll have the time of your life! I'll be here to guide you."

Resisting would be fruitless, so he raised one hand high and placed his other at her waist like the couple in front. In seconds they were stepping smartly in lines, twirling and spinning. "Hang on!"

"Don't worry, most don't know the steps to the Sir Roger de Coverley either. It's easy as the caller says what to do. The bluegrass reel resembles a tale of a fox on a hunt, and the object is to stay ahead."

Above the noisy partying, the dance caller, Klegg, echoed out over a speaker. "Two lines of ten couples, please! In turn, you will cross diagonally from one line to the top of the other."

"Here hand in hand, the boys unite,
And form a very pleasing sight.
Then through each other's arms, they fly,
As Thread does through the Needle's Eye."

As their feet fluttered together in and out, it made no sense to Bradley, but he didn't remember when he had laughed this hard.

"Step faster," Gabby said, "then run through the arch of arms and find me again."

As they twirled, he caught the eye of his father holding a fiddle on stage, creating a snapshot moment he'd remember, then Gabriella yanked him back into the dance.

"You're a spitfire, Gabby!"

"I suspect the bandleader is your dad as there's a striking similarity. It's quite the coincidence he's here tonight, don't you think?"

"Yes, he is. I was bold enough to place a wish in the box when I arrived, and someone apparently brought him here with the intent that we find each other. But we both know who would do that!"

"Dad makes the impossible possible, Brad."

"With his plans and conspiracies, he makes dreams come true."

"Are you happy tonight?"

"Gabby, I have never been more content than standing here this moment."

Dozens outside the circuit raised libations in toasts, swinging their arms and hips as they waited for turns in the dance queue.

Sadie nudged Rudy, seeing Lola and Cliff sitting close together. "Right there is proof that the Wishes and Deeds are fully in play. Seeing so many come together gives me ticklish pleasure."

Mandy's eyes widened at the ladies' costumes as they danced lightly past their table.

"Your face is glowing in the ceiling lights," her mother said.

Mandy twisted her fingers in her crimped ringlets and ribbons. "Mother, am I too young to have a chance?"

William Jackson turned to her. "Of course not, Mandy. I'd be honored to be your partner in the next round. Did I tell you how elegant and charming you look in your new dress?"

Mandy's shoulders rose as she giggled with excitement, and her smile spread ear-to-ear. "Ooh, are you sure? I might step on your toes."

But eager and impetuous, she jumped to her feet to oblige William.

"You may dance on my toes; I'm just happy to be here and to meet such a fine young lady. My father told me what a special companion you have been during my absence. That was exceptionally kind, Mandy."

He patted his father. "I'm glad you got me home in time to dance with my best girl, Dad."

Mr. Jackson was at last beginning to find the seasonal spirit, enjoying himself for the first time since his sons had enlisted. He held out his hand to Mrs. Carson. "Well, Maureen, shall we join the kids?"

Rudy and Sadie meandered with their greetings along the outer circle of seated guests, shaking hands and watching for a specific person.

"I was looking for you, Nate," he said, stopping suddenly. "Mandy gave me the excellent news, and I know who to thank for making her wish come true. A small girl's faith in Santa Claus is alive, and a family is reunited. It's an incredible gift!"

"Rudy, it was my destiny that day to be in the Emporium. Besides blessing these two families, it was an experience that I cannot put in words. I found part of myself, the purest belief in people and goodwill."

Nate's voice wavered, and a tear stung at his eye. "I see more than ever that Human kindness is endless; I believe again in Santa Claus."

Mrs. Newman was touched by her husband's release of emotion and recognizing his nod, she whisked him away. "Dear, it's time for us to join the dance line."

As the music softened, Klegg announced the band's break. "To all our Fezziwig guests, come again to the feasting tables. Load up your plates of cakes and sweets and refresh your drinks. Rest your feet and greet your neighbors. Fill yourselves, ha-ha, but don't anyone dare to mention your weight."

Philip Grayber seized an opportunity to approach Rudy. "I don't want to impose on the band, but I overstepped myself and encouraged young Benedict to bring along his violin tonight. Could he possibly play a Christmas tune? He's your town's protégé, and I know it would give him a boost of confidence."

Rimble overheard it and turned to a bandmate. "Come over here, Clarence, and bring your violin."

Clarence was soft-spoken, a tall, lean fellow with boney shoulders and scraggy hair. He removed a treasured instrument from a tapered violin case on the stage and strolled to Rimble to join the discussion.

"Rudy, this is Clarence. We've been together for a long time. Although we focus on the jigs and swing for your event, he is a skilled musician. I heard him play a classical number the other day, and I say a duet would thrill the crowd. Bring your lad up here, and we'll let him have a go at Clarence."

"If he's not fussy about his partner, I'd be honored," said Clarence.

"Let me have a word with Justin," Grayber said but gasped at his faux pas. "I'm sorry, I mean Benedict." As he left, Rudy explained.

"No apologies are necessary," said Rimble. "A family member's loss affects us forever. If this is meaningful to Mr. Grayber and Benedict, it's important to us."

The buffet had lost its popularity, and Clarence and Benedict began a fast-paced reel without an introduction. As Lydia watched the duo, she was overcome with emotion and squeezed Philip's hand.

"You don't know how much this means. You are a wonderful man, and I'm thankful and happy you came to Chimney Ridge to bless us. Benedict will always remember this night."

"I'll never forget this either, Lydia!"

With Mr. Klegg's proclamation for the last call at 1 a.m., Bradley needed a long talk with his father. "Dad, let me help pack up while we chat."

"Sure, son. I'm glad to see that you are safe and well. It is indeed a miracle for me tonight."

"I've been around these parts for a bit. But a few weeks ago, Mr. Hancock found me in a bus shelter during a storm and took me in as an elf in training that changed my life." He grinned at the scenario.

"He has obvious respect for you, Bradley, and you for him."

"Rudy taught me life lessons and helped me realize how foolish I was to storm out of our house when I did. I've wanted to go back many times, but with foolish pride, I didn't know how to deal with it."

"I've got some years of life experience under my belt, so let me help you with this. I know that elves work right until Christmas Eve, so what if I came back that night and took you home for Christmas? That gives you a few days to think and finish your obligations. Your mother will be thrilled to have you home."

Bradley stared at his father, seeing this wise man in a different light.

"Thank you, Dad! That's what I needed you to say."

22

Christmas Truck from New York

In the afterglow of the Fezziwig, townsfolk spoke of nothing but the thrill of the night's revelry.

With Christmas Eve days away, the Emporium's buzz of activity intensified. The basement workshop was elbow to elbow, sorting the Wishes and Deeds and matching the list provided from the mitten distribution at the church tree, with assignments to account for each one.

"Rudy, do we dare ask for more volunteers?" Sadie asked.

"No, we have a few more days. Bradley and Gary organized a crew to help, and Reverend Atkins will send a committee from the church.

"Just watch the energy that people put into these final days!" Rudy announced to Grayber. "It's time for everyone to deliver now, and they love it!"

"I see that. But who manages all the orders for toys?"

"Walter Hoskins is coordinating them. Bradley double-checks pickups and addresses to ensure that every delivery will be on time. Cliff's swap shop is polishing and sharpening skates."

"Hoskins, I see," said Grayber. "Do we need any more bicycles?"

"The town's mechanics are assembling all the bikes in a warehouse by the arena. We have red ones, blue, three-wheelers, and racers. They're beauties, I tell you!"

"You've figured it all out, Rudy."

"It's the whole town and brings the most fantastic feeling. The butcher and grocer are packing hampers today, and around Chimney Ridge, sewing machines are chugging, and ovens are pumping out trays of Christmas baking and gingerbread in all shapes.

Dozens of past years' recipients revisited the Emporium as Christmas to respect the traditions, including Nate Newman and his daughter Emmeline.

Suddenly a wave of compassion overcame Nate. "Emmeline, if you have any last request for Santa, this is the right mailbox."

"Yes, please, Daddy, I would like a puppy this year."

"A puppy? You've never told me that."

"I didn't want to ask for anything. You said you had everything you needed already, and I got to thinking it would be selfish of me to ask for something else."

Newman nodded, knowing her selfless character. "Dear Emmeline, children are encouraged to make a wish at Christmas."

"Why, Daddy? Why for children?"

"It gives them hope to look forward to, with belief in Santa and the elves that work so hard. If children didn't send wishes, Santa wouldn't have so much enjoyment on Christmas Eve. Elves are probably wondering why you hadn't asked."

"Oh, no, Dad, I went ahead and put one of those letters in Mr. Hancock's box. That way, if I do get a puppy, I'll know that Santa sent it. If I just asked you, then I wouldn't know for sure. Mandy Carson put her letter in that same box, and she got her wish already!"

Emmeline's youthful maturity inspired Nate. "Shall we get inside the Emporium and see what antics the elves are up to today?"

Gary and Bradley were assigned to shuttle goods to distribution points and pick up new Wishes and Deeds still needing attention.

Bradley picked up a pair of kittens for a family at the animal shelter and arranged for a dalmatian puppy that Santa would deliver to the Newman household.

While the boys were gone, a convoy of trucks with horns tooting and cabs decorated in white Christmas lights pulled up to the Emporium. Rudy ran out at the commotion, finding Philip Grayber in the driver's seat of the first truck.

"Merry Christmas, Rudy!" he shouted from the open window. "A Merry Christmas!"

"What the heck is this, Philip?"

Grayber was giddy with his surprise. "I have deliveries for Chimney Ridge from my New York warehouse. I met the trucks at the edge of town. If you direct me to your loading bay, then afterward, I'll need to find Hoskins."

"We hadn't ordered anything from Grayber Enterprises, Phil. What do you have?"

"Christmas is supposed to bring you surprises," Phil said.

"I'll drive to the back lane if you can open your doors."

Rudy made his way to the loading dock, baffled about the delivery. "Micah, we need help unloading, and when Gary and Bradley return, send them back as well!"

Grayber swung down from the cab. "Before I open the padlock, let me explain. I admit that the Fezziwig stirred my soul more than I expected."

"I'm happy about that, Phil."

"And I see that this town is inspired by music and dance, so in thinking about that, I decided that Chimney Ridge should have its own bluegrass band. Set in the middle of Vermont, you need one to be sure."

"I'm astonished at your intuition," said Rudy. "There's indeed talent in town that has yet to discover itself."

"You allowed young Benedict Thompson to realize a new dream, playing fiddle with Clarence at that level. It was heart-rendering, to say the least, and I'm grateful."

"We're all proud of Benedict, and it was appropriate to showcase his talent."

"Best of all, Rudy, I found a soulmate I met many years ago at my son's deathbed. I am heartened and have changed my life, replacing the sadness of the past. I could never repay the town for opening my eyes to this charitable spirit of Christmas."

Grayber was now standing on the truck's rear bridge.

"I am donating a full complement of band instruments to your local high school, and I've secured an agreement with a Concord music teacher to come and become the resident instructor."

"Instruments and a band too!" Rudy exclaimed. "It's all unbelievable!"

"One more important thing; my company will fund the

building of a youth hostile to provide care and comfort to lost and lonely travelers. It's a Christmas gift and won't be a burden to the town."

Grayber rolled up the rear door, revealing stacks of crates. His voice cracked, and his eyes teared as he spoke. "I feel like Santa today, and it's a remarkable feeling, Rudy."

"I can't believe this generous gift to our town, and I don't understand why you brought them here to the Emporium."

"In my idle time in your store, I did a number of sketches. As a result, I had the opportunity to capture the faces and hearts of your town."

"We did see you sketching, my friend."

"I contacted my creative department in New York," Grayber said. "We have a shipment of Fezziwig dolls today, exclusive to Hancock's Emporium. I brought ten dozen for you for now, and we'll send more when you're ready."

Rudy gasped. "Ten dozen Fezziwig dolls?"

"We also designed a child's fiddle with an instruction book for ambitious learners in keeping with the musical theme. So you see, I have a workshop too!"

Sadie flushed with pleasure. "Could I see one of the dolls?"

"Right away, Sadie." Grayber climbed into the truck back and opened a box. The first ones out were in the likenesses of the elves from the Emporium.

"Oh, Rudy, they have names," Sadie said. "Here's Micah! And there's Bradley! Oh, look, this one is certainly you. They are breathtaking. I'll start a collection to add to my favorite nutcrackers."

"The ultimate toy is the Fezziwig and Mrs. Fezziwig," Grayber said. "I based them on the principle of a spinning top and applied flexible umbrella struts. When one forces pressure on the plunger, the outfits fly open and twirl with the top."

Grayber laughed so hard at the vision in his mind that he had to rest on a crate.

"I'll register the copyright to Hancock's Emporium if you agree as they'll be considered collectibles, I'm certain. These dolls will provide revenue that can support the town's charitable needs. When the town can manage a factory, we can build it here and provide future employment if Leadner and his council agree. Of course, I will contribute to Chimney Ridge too in the future."

Grayber reached into a second box. "These are fantastical, don't you think?"

First, he took out Mrs. Fezziwig and set the point of it on the floor. On top of the spinner was the dancer's head of Mrs. Fezziwig, with a feather spire protruding from her bouffant.

As he pressed the spire a full depth, the top spun, and the struts of Mrs. Fezziwig's skirts flew out from the umbrella's folds and twirled above her dancing shoes.

Sadie doubled over with pleasure as the spinning top was a blur of skirts and feet, catapulting itself across the floor. "I've never imagined a toy this incredible. Both young and old will want these as souvenirs of the ball."

Rudy's eyes darted back and forth as they did in his most reflective manner, but he hadn't said a word as he was deep in creative thought and overcome by the demonstration.

"What do you think, Rudy?" Grayber asked.

"I couldn't envision such a great deed to befall our town. You are Chimney Ridge's benefactor, and the town should build a statue in your honor for the dedication you have shown!"

"Thanks are not necessary. Chimney Ridge gave me the gift of finding Christmas, and I now understand goodwill. Best of all, I have a family after so many years."

He whispered to Sadie, "She said yes, and we'll be married on New Year's Eve."

Sadie smiled so hard she felt her face would crack, and tears streamed on her cheeks.

"Is this a secret?"

"Perhaps you could let Lydia tell you herself." Grayber kissed Sadie's cheek, and she blushed in the joy of the moment.

From another colored box, Grayber produced a Fezziwig puppet, holding the body by its stick backbone, then pulled out more. Some had sticks and strings, and others had hand inserts, but each resembled one of Philip's sketches from the night of the ball.

"Philip Grayber, you are the master of toys to have these created," said Sadie. "A pure magician. I can tell from the costumes which ones they are!"

"I like to draw, and my designers understand my work. Although they are exclusive to Chimney Ridge, if you decide to distribute them otherwise, royalties would come into your coffers."

As Sadie pushed the plunger, the Fezziwig top whirred and hummed and spun across the floor with its colorful skirts and feet flying high in the air.

23

December 23rd

Grayber hopped back into the cab in a flash and started up the diesel engine. "I'll take the rest of the load to Hoskins Hardware. I gave Walter a heads up, and he's arranged for Metcalfe's school bus to help. We have aboard our most popular toys, and every child in need in town shall have one for Christmas. Hoskins will prowl the streets with the blowhorn to make the announcement."

"I'm flabbergasted, Phil, and that rarely happens to me," said Rudy. "My Pops would never have dreamed that someone could fulfill our Wishes and Deeds in this generous way."

When Mr. Metcalf pulled up in the afternoon with the school bus, a melee of customers was outside the Emporium, curious about the convoy and the excitement inside the store.

"Christmas won't wait, folks," Metcalf said. "See Mrs.

Hancock or Micah inside, and you can help us load the bus if you're inclined."

A strapping teen called back, "From the trucks?"

"You're right, young man. Red tags go to the back of the bus, yellow to the middle, and the green and blue tags get stacked in the front. Mr. Hoskins will manage the distribution, and the church folks will take care of the tree mitten requests."

Within twenty minutes, the bull horn was patrolling the downtown and venturing into side streets, announcing the special event at Hoskin's Hardware.

"A very Merry Christmas to you!" Mrs. Hoskins declared to the parents and snow-suited children that poured into the store, greeting each customer by name with candy cane bags at the door.

Philip Grayber's and Lydia Thompson's arms were intertwined as they strolled on the opposite sidewalk, and her head leaned to his shoulder.

"Phil, I'm so content at this moment," she said.

"I'm the same, dear Lydia."

She nodded at the flocks of kids outside Hoskins. "This is incredible! I'm glad you're here for many reasons, and having you with our family for Christmas dinner is a gift that's beyond my dreams. For five years, it's just been Benedict with me, and we've lacked companionship. It was my fault; I never thought I'd be ready. So I guess we have that Wish Box to thank."

"Is it a coincidence that the Von Trapp housekeeper directed me here? I wonder, and I definitely must thank her. Oddly, in all the years I've been to Stowe to ski at Justin's favorite place, I never found my way to this town."

They settled on a bench to gaze longer at the activity across the street.

With a final bite of Sadie's beef stew, Bradley knew it was time to talk. It was already late in the evening of December 23rd, the night before Christmas Eve. He rested his elbows on the Hancock's table, ready to broach the subject of leaving Chimney Ridge. It was his new dilemma, not unlike the one when he arrived in town.

He nodded his approval of the advent calendar across the room, watching the door for Christmas Eve that was yet to open. Each day had revealed a surprise, and he knew there would be only one more.

"Rudy, Sadie! I've decided to go back to see my parents in Concord for Christmas." He looked away rather than deal with disappointment on their faces. "I'll miss the opening of these calendar doors as they've inspired me each day."

"There's no reason for stress," Rudy said. "Every elf has left us on their Christmas Eves. We are thrilled that you found your family, and in that way, you also discovered yourself."

Sadie patted Bradley's hand. "If you had wanted to stay, of course, it would have pleased us equally. You are part of our family and made enormous contributions to our town."

Rudy went to the turntable and set it for 'White Christmas' to play softly.

"This song was playing the night that you arrived, so it's appropriate that you hear it again. As you've heard me say many times, Bradley, things happen for a reason."

"I see that now, sir."

"The sequence of events is fascinating. Why did our regular band cancel in the first place? Then, through references, I spoke with your father. It seemed coincidental, and I didn't immediately make the connection. After a bit of research, I realized that destiny was at play.

"In the Wish Box, I found a request that suited you, and everything fell in place, including your father's group. Fate had intended for both of you to be in Chimney Ridge."

Gabriella bounced into the kitchen and settled in the next chair. Bradley blushed as she wriggled her arm through his elbow, then twisted her head mischievously to look squarely into his eyes. "Did you have a good time at the Fezziwig?

Before he could say, she declared, "I'll be more than happy to have you as my dance partner another time. I hope you'll find a good reason to return at Christmas in the future."

Sadie relished Gabby's teasing banter and gently swatted a tea towel at her.

"Oh, yes, I'll be back," Bradley said with a grin. "My father will take me back home tomorrow for Christmas, but there's more. Remember Mr. Grayber's announcement as the benefactor of the high school music department? After the Fezziwig, my father has given Grayber his interest in helping to establish the music school."

It was Rudy's turn to be baffled. "Dang! You mean I've been out of the loop on this?" He patted his belly.

"So I may come here often with my father. Cliff Winters said he might have rooms to rent from time to time. He is working on some bigger idea."

"Then we'll see you from time to time," Sadie said. "Knowing your departure was imminent, I've been struggling to have to say goodbye. I'm like a Mama dog who hates when her pups leave but happy they have new homes."

"Christmas wouldn't be the same if I were far from

Sadie picked up the phone on the first ring. "It's Cliff Winters, Sadie! I need to talk to Rudy right away!"

"He's right beside me, Cliff."

She whispered as she handed the phone, "He sounds out of breath and anxious."

"Is something the matter, Cliff?" Rudy asked.

"It's not really what you would call a problem, but if you could lend an ear, I need your opinion. Do you mind stopping by my place?"

Rudy glanced at his family waiting for an update and cupped his hand over the receiver. "I need to see him," he mouthed.

"Cliff, I'll be along in a few minutes. Is there something you need me to bring?"

Rudy snatched his parka and dashed out the back door, cutting through lanes and rear driveways. Plodding through the unshovelled snow, he rounded the front veranda to find Cliff waiting at the front door.

"Are you sure you're alright, Cliff? It's late, and I thought you'd be gone to bed by now."

"I'm quite fine, Rudy. Come in!"

It had been many months since Rudy had stepped inside the Winters' home, and the loneliness struck him.

"Where's your Christmas spirit, Cliff? You have no tree or music and no cards hanging over the archway."

"I've noticed that myself, Rudy. You're the closest person I have to call a best friend." Cliff fidgeted and paced.

"You've seen in recent weeks that I've built an attachment to a certain lady."

"You must mean Lola Turnbull. We have noticed, and we hope everything will work out for both of you. But surely you don't need me to help you with that."

Cliff sagged into the opposite armchair. "You can see from my housekeeping and lack of homey touches that a woman wouldn't find my arrangement appealing. Quite a bit of Thelma still hangs in the air. I love that, but I know it's time to move on. I've been a widower for more than a year, and Lola needs me now. And Otis too."

Rudy nodded to himself and strolled through the main floor rooms making mental notes of furniture and needed alterations.

"We've received a proposal for a homeless shelter in Chimney Ridge," said Rudy. "If you have excess furnishings, I'm sure they would be grateful."

"Oh, I'm all for that," said Cliff.

"And I hope you don't mind me saying that the parlor room that Thelma used could be renovated and redecorated. As Lola has arthritis, this could be your master bedroom. Otherwise, I would defer to Lola's ideas for the rest of the house. Bradley tells me you might have rooms upstairs to let from time to time. That's a good idea to have a bit of brawn around on occasion."

Cliff nodded at the suggestion, putting Rudy at ease.

"I've yet to propose to Lola; our romance has developed quickly, but time is of the essence. I hope you and Sadie will help us arrange a small wedding either here in the house or in the tearoom. Most of our dates have been there. Very simple, with just the Reverend, our closest friends, and Otis."

"You don't need help then, Cliff, but I'll ask Sadie to stop over with pointers to make the house more appealing. It would be best if you started with flowers and perhaps a box of chocolates. However, do let us know what Lola says."

"Where can I get flowers at this hour?"

Cliff debated calling Lola or just going straight to her apartment to say what was burdening him.

At 9:30 p.m., he arrived at the security intercom and rang up. He thought her voice sounded sleepy, but she insisted that was not the case and released the lock.

Lola eased the door open, wearing a pink popcorn chenille robe. Cliff was leaning on one leg, holding a potted poinsettia, nervous and hoping not to look foolish.

"Cliff, how nice of you!"

"May I come in for a few minutes?"

"Of course, you're always welcome here."

Otis immediately recognized Cliff, sniffed his pant leg, then wiggled and wagged, luring him to crouch with ear rubs.

"Shall I fix something to eat or drink, Cliff?"

"No, Lola, I need to talk to you." He pushed the poinsettia toward her.

"I'll use them until I need to move, then perhaps you could look after the plant for me."

"We need to talk about that. Sit down, Lola; it will be easier."

"Easier! It sounds like you have something bad to tell me."

"Oh, no, nothing bad; I certainly hope not."

Flustered, he took a deep breath and pulled up at the kitchen table beside Lola.

"What's the matter, Cliff? You can tell me anything." He

reached for her hand, and she didn't pull away.

"I know that. A while ago, when we volunteered at the retirement lodge, I knew you were having a hard time with the entire situation. I said it would be alright and asked you to trust me, do you remember?"

"I thought you were gallant to ease my burden."

"I've given this a great deal of thought, and I have no hesitation in my decision. Lola Turnbull, in these last weeks, I have fallen in love with you. You're my last vision at night, and in the morning, you're my first thought. In between, I don't sleep well, and it's lonely. So if you and Otis will have me, I'd like to marry you."

The color drained from Lola's face as her hand came up to her lips. "I don't know what to say. There's so much to think about."

"Everything is trivial. I only need to know that you love me too, and all that matters will fall into place." He reached into his pocket for a small velvet box. "I've been carrying this around for several days, and I decided I couldn't go to sleep tonight unless I asked you."

Otis could see that Lola was overcome and put his paws on her lap, trying to get to her tears to soothe her. She kissed the top of his head then turned to Cliff.

"Yes, Cliff, I've found that I love you too."

It wasn't awkward at all as he took her hand and pulled her to her feet, and kissed her tenderly. They stayed in one another's arms for a long time.

24

Christmas Eve – Wishes and Deeds Fulfilled

On the afternoon of Christmas Eve at the Thompson house, Lydia and Philip finished stuffing the turkey, set it in the oven, and started on the vegetables.

"My sister, Helen, and her husband will be here at four, and we have to wrap a few more gifts before then. I haven't seen their three youngsters since they were babies. It's been a long time since I had a house full of guests for Christmas dinner."

"It's been even longer for me to join a family dinner," said Philip. "You do realize, Lydia, that I decided to be brave with a wish in the box to be included in a family celebration this year. Did Santa Claus whisper in your ear?"

"I believe that Santa whispered in Benedict's ear, then urged me about the seniors' lodge. I'm so grateful that happened, Phil. You've been a godsend to so many, but mostly to me. I knew when I saw you again at the Emporium that you were my soul mate."

"We belong together," Grayber said. "The three of us."

In the mid-afternoon, Keith Rimble pulled up to the Emporium in a Dodge van. A gift was on the seat beside him, wrapped with a green and gold ribbon tied both ways into a bow. He and his wife had been careful with their selections.

"Why should I feel nervous meeting the Hancocks again? They have embraced Bradley and changed him forever."

As he approached the entry, Eleanor Partridge barreled down the street and opened the door, pushing past him, but Rudy spotted him through the window.

"Ah, come on in, Keith. So you've come to collect our elf!"

"It's good to be back, Rudy. Merry Christmas!"

"Come upstairs. Sadie is helping Bradley get organized with a few things."

Hearing their voices, Sadie met them at the top. "Keith, you won't recognize me without my party costume, but I'm Sadie Hancock. We're glad to have you in our home. Bradley is in his room finishing the packing."

"There's no hurry," Keith said. "I'm glad you're both here. I brought this gift to show my appreciation for how you have watched out for my boy. Bradley explained how you taught him about giving, and I contemplated that thought at home. So I wish to give you this; you could say it is the life of Bradley the Elf."

Sadie removed a photo album from the gold foil wrapping, and as she turned the pages, she saw a sequence of Bradley's pictures from a young age, many at Christmas.

She quietly pored over them one by one until she came

to a teenager. "I see a sudden change here in Bradley. Then a gap until this year when you have several at the Fezziwig with him happy and letting his hair down again. So you have captured the full circle. This is a remarkable gift, Keith."

She passed the book to Rudy, who studied the changes in Bradley from a youngster in Coventry to a young man.

"We're thankful that you loaned him to us these last weeks. He has become part of our family and an integral part of the community in this short time. Did he happen to mention little Mandy Carson, who believes he is an actual elf?" Sadie said with pride.

They all turned as Bradley burst into the living room with his duffle. "Father, I didn't hear you arrive."

"We've been reminiscing about Bradley the Elf. You'll be missed here, son," said Rudy.

Bradley looked with hesitation at Sadie and Rudy. "I guess I'm ready to go then, Dad. But it seems I have one more delivery on our way out of town." He gestured to a package under his arm. "I've got Mandy Carson taken care of right here; it was a canceled wish but nonetheless a wish."

From the hall bureau, Sadie pulled out a wrapped gift. "Bradley, this is for you to open Christmas morning under your tree."

"And this is for your tree," he said with a grin, producing an envelope from his pocket. "I heard this is the way it all started with your Pops, Rudy."

"I don't know what to say, Bradley," said Rudy, but the shake in his voice let his vulnerability show. "You've touched my sore spot."

Starting with Sadie, Bradley leaned into each of them with heartfelt hugs. He didn't want to leave this moment and closed his eyes to remember the fragrance of Sadie's hair and the brush of Rudy's whiskers.

As the downstairs door closed, Sadie shivered like the first night when Rudy went out to find Bradley. A flood of December memories surged through her thoughts, and she felt strangely empty.

"Where are Gabriella and Gary?"

"You don't mind, Dad, if we go to Chestnut Lane? The little girl needs this elf to deliver something from Santa."

"You'll go through the chimney?" Keith teased.

"My cohort, William Jackson, next door, will ensure the delivery is made. Sometimes even Santa needs extra help."

The young soldier was watching for Bradley and met him by the fence.

"This is the cut-out book that Mandy asked Santa for in New York. I'm glad I met you at the Fezziwig, William. Your father will have a happier Christmas with you home."

"Mrs. Carson is hosting us for Christmas dinner tomorrow, and Dad and I have a few other gifts for the family. She told me about Mandy's wish, and I figured that was how I came to be home."

William patted Bradley on the back. "I don't know who is directly responsible, but I'd like to believe, like Mandy, that Santa got her letter."

25

Gratitude & Unity

Early morning lights flickered across Chimney Ridge on Christmas morning as children dug deep into stockings filled with candy and fruit and squealed at retrieving their parcels from under the tree.

Carl Bench's voice came on with the 6:00 a.m. news, and when Gary heard the beginning of the announcement, he flipped to another station as he had agreed. Carl's message and tone were vigorous.

"Good morning and Merry Christmas to the fine folks of Chimney Ridge. I have a special plea to everyone who benefited from a wish granted or was the recipient or donor of a deed this year or any other for that matter.

"This is simple. All you have to do is file down Main Street and be outside Hancock's Emporium at eleven o'clock this morning. We'll show gratitude to the Hancock family, who have given of themselves, bringing the Christmas spirit to Chimney Ridge and building our town's charitable character. There isn't a soul that can deny any benefit from their labors. Let's unite and show them our appreciation!"

Phones rang, and chatter stirred throughout the town as residents organized themselves to assemble on Main street.

Sadie's traditional Christmas breakfast of fluffy German pancakes was hot from the oven, and she adorned them with dollops of fresh fruit and whipped cream, sides of bacon, and sausage. Rudy perked her favorite dark roast coffee, and Gary refilled the orange juice. Unwinding from the month's pace, the Hancocks were simply rejoicing at being together.

"Bradley must be enjoying his Christmas back at home at last," said Gary. "I got used to him as a roommate and hope I'll see him again sometime."

Gabriella poked her brother. "Don't forget your sister is right here, and you haven't seen her in months."

He was used to her sarcasm. "I'm glad to have this time with you, Sis, but you see, there is something that only us guys understand. Merry Christmas!"

"Merry Christmas," she howled. "I have missed you too."

With a glint in his eye, he said. "Have we opened all our presents? Dad, did you check the tree thoroughly?"

Curious that Gary was toying with him, Rudy pushed his chair back from the table and moseyed to the tree.

"Remember how Pops hid envelopes in the branches?" Gary prodded.

"Ha, ha!" Rudy said, continuing to rifle without success.

"A bit lower," Gary said. "The height of a child, hiding something for his father."

Spying a faded piece of paper, Rudy was startled to see his own handwriting as a boy. 'To Pops.'

He read the sentiment to himself, then plopped into an overstuffed armchair with his eyes twinkling with tears.

> Dear Pops,
> As you have taught us to give of ourselves, I don't have a wrapped present for you, but I give you my whole heart. You can have endless hugs and ask me to stand by you through anything. On your behalf, I gave my whole bank account $4.87 to the soup kitchen. Merry Christmas!"
> Love, Rudy.

Underneath the signature were the words, 'Gary, forever,' and a small note from behind fell to his lap. He read the message and glanced at his watch.

"Why, it's ten to eleven already."

"Wait until the church bells ring for exactly eleven, Dad," Gary said.

Sadie eased forward and took the papers to read, then at the kitchen table, the foursome held hands and waited. Finally, at eleven, Gary turned the radio back on, tuning in to Carl Bench.

"Chimney Ridge, we are here on Main Street in front of Hancock's Emporium. Rudy and Sadie, if you're listening, go to your front door. It's our thank-you for all you have done, for the inspiration you have given our town so selflessly."

Sadie and Rudy held hands down the stairs, and even from inside the store, they could hear the noise and see the crush of townsfolk outside.

Rudy opened the door to applause and Carl with a remote microphone.

"Merry Christmas, Sadie and Rudy," Carl said, then turned to the crowd. "Now, I would like to ask these fine people who gathered here this morning to raise your hands if you have ever placed a wish or fulfilled a deed here at Hancock's. Now is the time to show your gratitude."

Cheers went up, and every hand raised. Suddenly a single voice from the sidewalk rose from the crowd, singing, 'We Wish You a Merry Christmas.' Quickly, others joined in spontaneously, with the thrill of their acapella voices carrying down the sidewalk, out onto the street, and down the block.

Sadie and Rudy knew every person in their sight. Old Mr. Jackson was waving from the sidewalk with William's arm over his shoulder, and next to them, Cliff Winters and Lola Turnbull were pressing against each other, bearing broad smiles.

Philip Grayber was cozy with Lydia Thompson and Benedict, chattering now like a family. They cupped their hands to their mouths when Rudy saw them and shouted out a Merry Christmas, drowned out by cheering up and down the street.

Nate Newman held up his new dalmatian pup, Henry Parker brought his shiny bicycle through the snow, and Sandra Davidson's polished skates hung over her shoulder.

Mrs. Middleton was elegant in her new feathered hat, and closest to the store, in front of all the townsfolk were Mrs. Carson and her children, clapping and waving.

But it was something else that Sadie noticed, that everyone was wearing colorful mittens.

Rudy stepped forward with Bench's microphone. "I can't find the words to express my thanks. I wish my father were standing here with me today, and I am grateful to be with my wonderful wife and two children who have stood by this dream of spreading goodwill. I have never been happier than at this moment as I see that many of you have been blessed."

Miles away in Concord, New Hampshire, the Rimble family shared a long-awaited Christmas morning, with any past sadness replaced with joy.

After breakfast, Bradley went to the parcel waiting under the tree, the one that Sadie and Rudy had given him. Tearing the paper off, he held a likeness of himself dressed in an Elf ensemble from Philip Grayber's sketches. He turned it around to read the manufacturer's tag: Chimney Ridge's Senior Elf, Bradley, prototype, and was deeply moved.

"Mom and Dad, this is an original collector's item that no one can ever replace. Some day, I'll pass it down to my own son or daughter. Merry Christmas!"

The End

"It is more blessed to give than to receive."
—Acts 20:35

Afterword

Several years ago, I was helping out at a community Christmas photoshoot, and my role was to record information from the lineup of families waiting to sit with Santa. I wore a red and green elf hat and a red cardigan to be part of the aesthetics.

Parents gave me the registration information, then nudged their children forward in the queue.

At one point, there was a lull, and I looked up to see a little blond curly-haired boy of not more than four years old staring at me with bright blue eyes. Then, gaining confidence, he eased forward and put his arms on the table, rested his chin, and gazed at me.

He whispered so no one else would hear, "Are you an elf?"

At that moment, I was aware that he genuinely thought that I was, and my reply would be significant to this young boy.

I put my finger to my lips to indicate we would talk in confidence. "I am. Santa is so busy he dispatches many of his elves to all the places he has to be. I am lucky to be chosen to be here today, and I'm happy to be able to meet you."

"I thought so," he said with a nod. Then the line moved forward, and our moment passed.

I will never forget the look on his face and the belief in his heart. He was convinced he had just met an elf.

—Shirley Burton

About the Author

Shirley Burton is a Canadian author in fiction genres, including suspense thrillers in the Thomas York Series, old-fashioned whodunit capers in Inspector Furnace Mysteries, and nostalgic, family-oriented Christmas stories. Journey on her historical fiction from France in the 1500s, and let your imagination take you on the inspiring fantasy adventure *Boy from Saint-Malo*.

Shirley's residence is in Niagara-on-the Lake, Ontario, and Calgary, Alberta.

"I've been privileged to explore the locations of my books, walking the characters' neighborhoods and streets. Research has taken me to Istanbul, France, Italy, Greece, London, Amsterdam, Brazil, California, New York, and Quebec.

"Join me in my 600-page historical fiction, *Homage: Chronicles of a Habitant*, that portrays ten generations of a typical family migrating from France to the New World, paralleling real-world events over 500 years.

"There comes a time in life to take the leap into writing. It's that time for me."

Shirley Burton

shirleyburtonbooks.com

CLOCKMAKER'S CHRISTMAS

A nostalgic Christmas story for all ages. A mother of two small children travels from Manhattan to Heidelberg to resolve an estate. In the magical setting of the Castle and the Christmas markets, she is tempted into a whirlwind romance. With matchmaking charm, a clockmaker bestows unique gifts on the couple. A feel-good, old-fashioned Christmas.

A WENCESLAS CHRISTMAS

A Christmas story of love and charity in the French Alps near Chamonix at a centuries-old luxury hotel. Chef Marceau's niece catches the eye of the sous-chef, sparking a romance. Following an avalanche and a family isolated in the mountains, a spirit of charity grows at the hotel, inspired by tales of the Good King Wenceslas. Together, the employees and guests carry the Wenceslas spirit into the village.

CHRISTMAS TREASURE BOX

Polly Perkins operates the family antique shop. In the days before Christmas, she finds her grandmother's diaries, revealing a lost love she had held from others in her life. Polly meets a man who whisks her into a romance. A distant relative claims on the family's resources, and Polly pursues a resolution toward a memorable Christmas Day.

MYSTERY AT GREY STOKES

An Inspector Furnace Mystery, an old-fashioned whodunit in a Christmas setting. In an English country manor, during festivities, guests arrive for a splendid traditional feast. The cast includes the butler, housekeeper, the Berwick family members, and social guests. Inspector Furnace and Detective Prentice are called to the manor to untangle the deception and solve the case.

Printed in the USA
CPSIA information can be obtained
at www.ICGtesting.com
JSHW020453011024
70766JS00001B/40